Luckily for her, his eyes were shut, thick and long lashes resting against his manly cheeks. She took some moments to study his bronzed, muscular shoulders and chest which tapered into a lean waist. His chest was liberally sprinkled with curly hair, just enough to make a woman want to swoon into his arms. Feeling like a voyeur, Sia turned her head away to remove a large, fluffy towel to spread it over his chest. She lifted his open hair and piled it into a loose knot on the top of his head. "Can you tell me where exactly it hurts?"

When Ritvik pointed to the left side of his neck without opening his eyes, Sia said in warning, "I'm going to press an icepack to that spot," before placing it gently against the area and holding it there.

Ritvik gave a long and deep groan…

ABOUT THE AUTHOR

Sundari Venkatraman is an Indie Author who has 60 books to her credit. These books have consistently featured in the Top 100 Bestseller Lists on Amazon India, Amazon USA, Amazon UK, Amazon Canada and Amazon Australia in both romance as well as Asian Drama categories. Her latest hot romances have all been on #1 Bestseller slot in Amazon India for over a month.

MAHARAJA INTERNATIONAL is the third in The Bansal Legacy trilogy which are novels set in the background of 5-star hotels. This kindle book remained in #1 Bestseller position on Amazon India for more than ten weeks in the Contemporary Romance and Asian Drama categories.

Even as a child, Sundari absolutely loved the 'lived happily ever after' syndrome and she grew up on a steady diet of fairy tales, Phantom comics and Mandrake comics. It was always about good triumphing over evil and a happy ending after the protagonists surmounted all unexpected obstacles.

Once she entered her teens, Sundari switched her loyalties from fairy tales to Mills & Boon. While she loved reading both of these, she kept visualising what would have happened if there were similar situations happening in India; to local heroes and heroines. And of course, the joy of vanquishing the ubiquitous evil villains! Her imagination soared and she happily ensconced herself in a rosy romantic cocoon for many years.

Then came the writing—a true bolt from the blue! And Sundari Venkatraman has never looked back.

Books by Sundari Venkatraman

Standalone novels
The Malhotra Bride
Meghna
The Madras Affair
An Autograph for Anjali
Twin Torment
Finding Anya
Mr. Perfect
Man Friday
Her Prince Charming
Love in Agartha
Arjun's Penance
The Floundering Author
Once Bitten Twice Lucky
Ryan Finds a Bride
Tinder Loving Care
Shaan Gets Hitched
For Better or For Worse
Heartthrob
Call of the Heart

Collection of shorts
Matches Made in Heaven
Tales of Sunshine

The Groom Series Trilogy
#1 Groomnapped
#2 Gobsmacked
#3 Grounded

Dashavatar (Indian Mythology)
MATSYA: The First Avatar
KURMA: The Second Avatar
VARAHA: The Third Avatar
NARASIMHA: The Fourth Avatar
VAMANA: The Fifth Avatar
PARASHURAMA: The Sixth Avatar

The Writer's Toolkit (Non-fiction)
Publishing Your Book on Amazon KDP

Marriages Made in India Series
#1 The Runaway Bridegroom
#2 Her Smitten Husband
#3 His Drunken Wife
#4 Her Secret Husband
#5 The Casanova's Wife
#6 Her Bohemian Husband

The Bansal Legacy Trilogy
#1 Simha International
#2 Rose Garden International
#3 Maharaja International

Written in the Stars Series
#1 Scorpio Superstar
#2 Leo's Desire
#3 Taurus Temptation
#4 Virgo's Krush

The Thakore Royals Trilogy
#1 The Marriage Predicament
#2 Tied in Knots
#3 The Wooing of the Shrew

Romantic Shorts
#1 *Chahti Hoon Tumhe*
#2 Beauty is but Skin Deep
#3 Madeinheaven.com
#4 An Arranged Match
#5 The Reluctant Bride
#6 *Shweta ka Swayamvar*
#7 Papa's Girl
#8 Red Rose Dating Agency
#9 Rahat Mili
#10 Reema's Matchmakers
#11 The Matchmaker's Dream

**The Princess Series
(Historical Romance)**
#1 The Passionate Princess
#2 The Rebel Princess

THE BANSAL LEGACY
BOOK #3

MAHARAJA
INTERNATIONAL

SUNDARI VENKATRAMAN

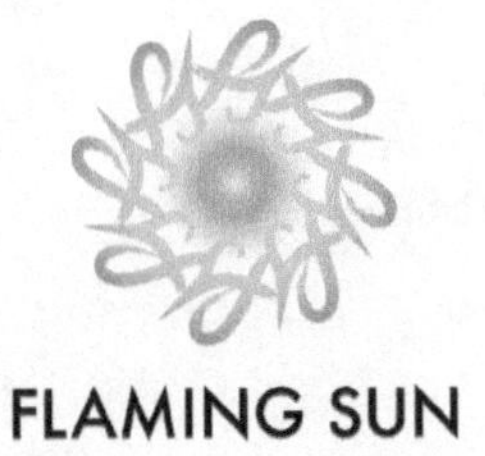

FLAMING SUN

Notion Press Media Pvt Ltd

No. 50, Chettiyar Agaram Main Road,
Vanagaram, Chennai, Tamil Nadu – 600 095

First Published by Flaming Sun 2017
Printed & Distribution by Notion Press
Copyright © Sundari Venkatraman 2022
All Rights Reserved.

ISBN 979-8-88783-559-4

Cover design by: Unaiza Merchant
Beta read by: Rubina Ramesh
Edited & marketed by: The Book Club

DEDICATION

This July birthday edition is for Vinitha, my daughter who is also my friend. We argue all the time. And it's from Vinny have I learned what unconditional love is all about! Thank you for being the best daughter in the world. Love you Vinny!

One of the things the hospitality industry offers is employment on every level. Whether someone just made the brave move from another country, with perhaps little education or with a lot of education and degrees crossing over from another industry, all of these folks have opportunities in tourism. Young or old, part time or full time, it needs everyone.

– Laurie Armstrong

ACKNOWLEDGEMENT

Thank you, **Varun Sood,** for talking to me! Thank you so much, **Lawyer Saumya Uma,** for clarifying the legal points for me. It was a great help indeed.

I would also like to thank the following people for all their help while I did the research for *The Bansal Legacy* series. (This was sometime in the year 2005)

Mr. Suresh Shetty, Director, Hotel Ashray International, Sion

Mr. Vithal Kamat, Chairman and General Manager, The Orchid, Vile Parle

The names and designations below are from 2005 when I did my research. These people must have moved on to bigger positions by now, I am sure:

- Ms. Rajul Semal, Environment Executive, The Orchid
- Mr. Vikas Kumar, Management Trainee, The Orchid
- Mr. Sachin Bhosle, Shift Engineer, The Orchid
- Ms. Aparna Desai, Housekeeping, The Orchid
- Mr. J. B. Singh, Senior Executive, Stores, The Orchid
- Mr. Shailesh, Asst. EDP Manager, The Orchid
- Mr. Gautam, Jr. Sous Chef, The Orchid

PROLOGUE

Ritvik Bansal grinned widely at his family—his parents, Alok and Menaka Bansal, his brother Rohit and sister-in-law Tasha, and his sister Rhea and brother-in-law Jamie. "I'm so glad you could all make it at such short notice. I…"

"What's up, Ritvik?" Rohit gave his brother a friendly slap on his shoulder. "You sounded urgent on the phone. All's well, I presume." His parents and sister nodded, looking a tad anxious, while Tasha and Jamie smiled at their mischievous brother-in-law. It was obvious that he had some good news.

"Have you got a girlfriend?" asked Jamie, with a wink.

"Something even better! Just hang in there for a minute and I'll be back with my good news." Giving them all a broad wink, Ritvik turned to walk out of the room and returned a few seconds later, wheeling a cradle into the room. "Meet my daughter Aarya who arrived into this world yesterday…"

Everyone's jaw dropped even as they stared at Ritvik and his baby with varying expressions of shock, horror and astonishment.

Barely seconds later, all began to talk at once. Menaka lifted her granddaughter into her arms, tears rolling down her cheeks. She turned away from her son, refusing to talk to him. But again, she didn't want to say anything harsh in the newborn baby's hearing, not about her father. It wasn't the little one's fault anyway.

Alok stared at his youngest born, torn between his love for him and his exasperation at the abrupt announcement, while a third part of his mind was also excited about the birth of a new generation. "How the hell did this happen? When did you get married?" Black eyes under bushy salt and pepper eyebrows glared at Ritvik.

"As I told you Pappa, Aarya was born yesterday. As for your other question, I didn't get married. My baby was born through traditional surrogacy and I'm a single father."

"But Ritvik," Alok's bushy eyebrows formed a straight line above his piercing eyes, "Why the hell would you do that? What's wrong with the usual way? And don't tell me you couldn't find a suitable woman for a wife. I wouldn't believe it." While he didn't interfere too much in his adult children's private lives, Alok Bansal was well aware of Ritvik's reputation as a ladykiller.

Ritvik looked into his father's eyes, his own black gaze unfathomable. "But that's the truth, Pappa. There's no woman that I want to marry."

Alok shook his head in vexation, throwing his hands up in the air. "I find that strange. How the hell do you plan to bring up a baby on your own? Damn it! Aarya needs a mother too." His frown grew heavier by the second.

Menaka walked further away from the arguing men, cooing to her granddaughter. But she made it clear through her body language that Ritvik deserved every bit of the scolding his father was meting out.

"I don't think so. She has me. I'll be both mother and father to her. And then there's Meera Aunty who has agreed to take care of Aarya along with me."

Alok looked behind Ritvik, noticing Meera for the first time. "What are you doing here in Udaipur, Meera? I thought you lived in Mahabaleshwar, taking care of the Sharmas' kids." Alok growled at the woman.

"The Sharmas' kids are all grown up. I am here to look after Aarya nowadays." Meera wasn't too worried by Alok Bansal's scowl. Though he had a booming voice, she knew for a fact that he had a heart of gold which he had passed on to all his children, especially his youngest.

"Since when?" The next question shot out from Alok.

"Two weeks."

Rhea jumped into the conversation, her eyes emitting sparks at Ritvik when she said, "So! Meera Aunty knew that you were going to have a baby before two weeks. How could you spring this on us as a surprise? Have you forgotten that we are your family? I never expected this of you, Ritvik." Her voice was reproachful as she punched his shoulder hard.

"Please Rhea." Ritvik hugged his sister or at least tried to, for she pushed him away. "This was the third attempt at surrogacy and it has finally succeeded. I didn't want to tell you guys until the baby was born. Please understand."

"No, I don't." Rhea buried her face against Jamie's shoulder, unable to stop her tears. The birth of a baby should be something one looked forward to; especially if the baby belonged to one's brother. But this was too shocking for words. She couldn't understand Ritvik's need for secrecy.

Rohit raised a fist as if to hit his younger brother who was all of twenty-nine. "Are you mad?" he asked Ritvik. "I agree with Pappa. What happened to the normal way of having a baby? I could understand if you were gay, but..."

Ritvik hugged his brother. "I don't ever want to be saddled with a wife," he declared, his voice completely devoid of emotion.

Unable to hold back any more, Menaka handed her baby granddaughter to Meera and gestured to her to take the baby to the bedroom before voicing her opinion. "How could you, Ritvik?" She spoke in a whisper to begin with but soon lost control as she held her huge son by his muscular arms and shook him. "How could you be so irresponsible as to bring an innocent baby into this world, depriving her of a mother? Do you really think that the role of a mother in a child's life is so negligible?" Unshed tears shone in Menaka's eyes as she glared at Ritvik.

"Oh Mamma!" Ritvik threw his arms around his mother, holding her close to his chest, rubbing his chin over the top of her head. "Please forgive me. I didn't mean to hurt any of you. And no, I don't think a mother's role is negligible." He held her by the shoulders to look down at her, pain in his own black gaze. "How will I think that after the way you brought us all up? But... can you understand that I needed to have a baby of my own? My own flesh and blood, someone to love and cherish?" He shook his head, stopping his mother from saying anything as he placed a finger on her lips. "I don't want to marry, ever. Pappa's lucky to have you. So are Rohit and Jamie as they have wonderful women for their partners. I'm obviously not meant to have a 'happily ever after'. Would you rather I missed being a father?"

Not really having an answer to that, Menaka hugged her son, drawing deep breaths to calm down.

It took them all the rest of the day to accept the status quo. And Jamie's and Tasha's presense helped as the two of them made light of the situation, switching the conversation to other subjects.

It wasn't long before the tightly knit Bansal family rallied together to welcome Aarya Bansal into their fold.

Sia Rathod was alone in the beauty salon in Maharaja International when Ritvik Bansal walked into Cleopatra's at 7.30 in the morning. The twenty-five-year-old had taken over the running of the salon at the 5-star hotel only the earlier day and wasn't yet familiar with the other employees.

Mischievous by nature, Sia was forced to curb her instinct to make some saucy comment, being a bit wary on unfamiliar territory for one thing. Secondly, perceiving that the man in front of her was beyond handsome, her heart had decided to take a leap into her throat and choke her. For God's sake, he wore a man bun which sat so well on his leonine head. His luxuriant beard made her hands itch to take a pair of scissors and have a go at taming it. His black eyes were set under thick eyebrows and were knife sharp. His hawk of a nose was perfectly centred. While his features were all hard planes and sharp angles, his lips were a dead giveaway to the softness which probably resided somewhere deep within. And that's what had ticked off Sia's heart—the combination of toughness and pliancy. He was clad in a pair of dark blue jeans and a black t-shirt which set off his broad shoulders and bulging muscles.

Of course, she had known her share of good-looking men, but never had Sia felt shaken by the mere presence of a man, and a stranger at that.

Unaware that she was talking to the Managing Director of the hotel, Sia cleared her throat and welcomed him as she would any other guest. "Hello sir! Good morning! How may I help you?" she asked with a smile on her piquant face.

"Hey, good morning!"

The man's smile was explosive as Sia's heart hammered in her throat, setting her pulse racing. Is this how one felt just before a heart attack?! She instinctively pressed a hand to her throat, hoping to calm down her pulse rate as she stared at the man stupidly, trying to comprehend his words.

"Are you new here?" He spoke again.

She blinked before nodding. "Yes sir."

"Sia," he read from the badge on her left shoulder, "Welcome to Maharaja International!" His smile turned to a grin as he put forth his hand to grasp her cold one before shaking it vigorously. "Where's everyone else?"

"They should be here by eight, sir. It was late when we packed up last night." Sia gave the stranger the explanation only because she had concluded by now that he was probably part of the management.

"And yet you're here on time," he complimented her. "By the way, I'm Ritvik Bansal."

Sia's mouth opened wide in an O. The client was none other than the owner of this popular heritage hotel set in the middle of the Udai Sagar Lake, in the heart of Udaipur. "Pleased to make your acquaintance, sir," she said, awe in her voice. He appeared so young. From what she had heard, he had built the hotel from scratch, renovating the rundown heritage property to the classy structure it was today.

Ritvik tilted his head in acknowledgement before saying, "Okay Sia. What I need is a trim, just my beard and sideburns. Do you think you can manage that?" The smile had disappeared and he was suddenly all business. "And I'm in a hurry."

"But of course, sir. Please take a seat." Sia pointed to one of the plush chairs in front of the mirrored wall. It looked as if her desire was going to be fulfilled almost immediately, the one of having a go at shaping his beard. With a smile on her face, Sia brought out a hair cutting cape and opened it with a flick of her wrists before wrapping it around his wide shoulders, snapping the single button closed at the back of his neck.

Ritvik watched her brief and efficient movements in the mirror, his eyes keen. Sia was not conventionally beautiful, her nose short and tip-tilted while her lips were a bit too generous and wide. Her smoky grey eyes which appeared almost silver were her most striking feature. She was busty with wide hips while her waist was small and her legs pretty long. Ritvik judged her to be about five feet, seven inches tall. She was dressed in black formal trousers and a white shirt. The red apron which she wore, bore the stylish profile of a crowned and bejewelled king—the hotel's emblem—in its centre. He couldn't but agree that the entire package was extremely attractive.

Sia took out an electronic beard trimmer and ran it efficiently over Ritvik's thick beard, from one end to the other, trimming away the excess with a minimum of fuss. Then she took out a pair of small scissors and comb from the pocket in her apron and shaped his sideburns to perfection. She quickly dusted the hair off his cheeks and shoulders before removing his cape. "Is that alright, Mr. Bansal?" She had a tough time keeping her eyes free of expression. He looked even more delectable than before.

"It's perfect, Sia. Thanks!" He got up and left abruptly, with a wave of his hand, leaving Sia to tend to her grumbling heart.

There was a reason for Ritvik's hurry. He was taking his daughter for her first ride on horseback. He rushed back to the King of Spades suite where he lived along with his two-year-old daughter Aarya, and the little girl's nurse, Meera, who was in her late fifties.

"Hello!" He called out, walking into the suite.

"Daddhieee!" yelled a baby voice, bubbling with joy. Aarya ran to her father and clung to his legs before he lifted her up into his arms.

"Good morning, princess. Have you had your breakfast yet?"

Aarya shook her head vigorously, the dark brown ringlets of her hair tumbling all over her face, her silver-grey eyes too large for her piquant face. "No Daddhie. I wanna eat with you. Afther horse ride," she lisped, before pressing her lips to his rough cheek.

Ritvik grinned at his adoring little girl, tweaking her retrousse nose as he shook his head at her. "Breakfast first. What do you want to have today?"

"Pizza," she grinned back, "with cheese."

Ritvik grin turned wider as he shook his head again. "Not in the morning, love. *Aloo paratha*?" He tilted his head to give her a mischievous look. "And we can have pizza for lunch. What say?"

"Yeth!" Aarya gurgled with laughter as her father tickled her stomach. "Daddhie, I love you."

"I love you too, imp." He kissed her soundly before carrying her out through the door. "Meera Aunty, I'm taking Aarya out. We'll get back by around 10 o' clock."

"Meera Aunty," Aarya took it upon herself to inform the lady, "I'm going outh with Daddhie."

"Bye sweetie. You enjoy your first ride on Pinnocchio." Meera gave her charge an adoring smile as she waved father and daughter off.

Father and daughter went to Jhansi ki Rani on the ground floor next to the entrance, the restaurant which served the local cuisine of Rajasthan. Deepak, the waiter, came rushing when he saw his boss enter the restaurant along with his daughter. He pulled two adjacent chairs out at their favourite table near the window before bringing forth a couple of cushions for the little girl. "Good morning, sir, Aarya. Shall I get you your favourite *aloo paratha*?" Deepak smiled at her charmingly.

"Yeth pleethe. Gu Mornin'." She nodded her head vigorously. "Milkshake too." She looked up at her father enquiringly.

Ritvik nodded in reply. "Mango?"

"I like mango."

"Okay." Ritvik turned to the waiter and said, "Good morning, Deepak. Have you taken Aarya's order?" When the waiter nodded, he continued, "I'll have two scrambled eggs with chickpea masala along with two plain *parathas* and coffee."

"I wanna egg," piped up Aarya.

"That's all, Deepak." Ritvik turned to his daughter and said, "You can have some from my plate."

"And you can have some *aloo paratha* from my plathe."

"Thank you, baby." Ritvik stretched a gentle hand to brush back the curls which fell over her eyes. The past two years had been extremely fulfilling. It wasn't the easiest of tasks, bringing up a child as a single parent, but it had been totally worth it. And then there was Meera Aunty who took care of the little girl when he was at work. Ritvik did manage to spend a lot of time with his daughter despite his busy schedule. He had even taken her to Mahabaleshwar to his parents' home; to Mumbai to stay with Rohit and Tasha and also to Ooty to spend time with Rhea and Jamie. Tasha was expecting a baby in the next month or so while Rhea was three months' pregnant. Ritvik grinned to himself. Aarya was going to have cousins to play with soon.

It had taken some time for Rhea to rally around. She had been furious with her younger brother for having had a child through surrogacy, especially because he had sprung it on the family as a surprise. But well, Ritvik couldn't imagine his family agreeing to this idea of his if he had told them before the event. Their anger, to his relief, hadn't lasted long being faced with little Aarya.

He truly enjoyed the fruits of being a father without being saddled with a wife that he didn't want.

"Daddhie." Aarya drew his attention to the food which Deepak placed on their table. She picked up the milkshake he had brought for her in a smaller glass and took a sip which formed a pale yellow moustache above her lips, grinning at her father, saying, "I also have *moochi* like you."

Ritvik laughed, nodding. "You do, and looking so cute too." He took his phone out and quickly clicked a couple of pictures and showed them to his little girl.

She wrinkled her nose at the picture and said, "Like Daddhie."

"Like Daddy. Now, let's eat our food before it turns cold. Pinocchio must be getting impatient." He had bought the foal a couple of months ago when the fairy tale character Pinocchio had been Aarya's favourite. And that's how the young horse had landed up with the name. Ritvik's words worked like magic now as Aarya was so looking forward to her first ride on her own horse which her father had gifted her when she turned two. He fed her a few titbits from his plate while Aarya insisted on stuffing pieces of *aloo paratha* into his mouth. He drew the line at sipping from her milkshake. "No, little one. I prefer to have coffee."

"Me coffee?" She tilted her head to look up at him appealingly.

"When you're older. Coffee isn't for babies."

"I'm a big girl, Daddhie. Noth baby," declared Aarya.

Ritvik paused, his coffee mug in his hand. Oh yes, she was growing up pretty fast, his little baby. "Not a baby, yeah. But still a little girl. You can have coffee when you're a big girl."

"Why?"

"Because tiny girls get tummy ache when they drink coffee."

"You no get tummy ache?"

"No."

"You are big boy." She nodded, satisfied with his reply, before finishing her milkshake. "*Chalo chalo.* Let's go. Pin'chio is waiting."

Ritvik laughed, ruffling her hair. "Sure, princess. Let's be off."

Not really known for his patience, Ritvik was the epitome of the virtue where his little girl was concerned. He seated Aarya on the small saddle customised to fit her, a cycling helmet on her head, her little feet tucked firmly into the stirrups. He held the reins in his left hand as he walked the horse slowly around the fenced paddock at the back of his hotel. He smiled every time he heard Aarya giggle, as she obviously enjoyed her first ride.

It was half an hour before he lifted the protesting child into his arms. "No Daddhie. I wanna ride Pin'chio some more," said Aarya, clinging to Ritvik's neck.

"I know sweetheart. But Pinocchio is still a baby and he's tired. I'm sure he's also hungry. Do you want to feed him an apple?"

Aarya's eyes went wide with wonder as she nodded vigorously. "Yeth. Lemme go. I'll go and get apple."

Ritvik let her down, holding her hand firmly. "Don't rush off. Let me do some magic." He shut his eyes, waved his hand in the air, and muttered some mumbo-jumbo, much to Aarya's delight. She danced around on her tiny feet, gurgling with glee as she watched her father in fascination, not noticing him dig into his voluminous jacket pocket before producing an apple. "Here you go," he said, handing the apple to her.

Aarya ran to Pinocchio and offered the apple to him. The horse opened its mouth and gobbled the whole apple at one go. Aarya laughed, clapping her little hands. "Daddhieee, Pin'chio ate apple."

"Yeah. He was obviously hungry." Ritvik held a hand out to Aarya and waited for her to hold him before he turned around to walk towards the heritage hotel which was to be their home until the cottage beside it—a structure which used to house the royal kitchens in yonder days—was renovated to become their new home. Aarya skipped along with her father, content and happy with her lot, not knowing enough to miss a mother in her life.

S ia was in a dreamy state since that morning, after her encounter with the big boss. While she had been extremely thrilled to land the job of the salon manager at Maharaja International, meeting Ritvik Bansal had thrown her completely off kilter.

Until a couple of weeks ago, it had been her dream to run a salon. Sia had worked really hard to get where she was today. She had been excited when she was called for the interview and subsequently selected for the job. It was truly a feather in her cap for the small-town girl hailing from the historic district of Dholpur in Rajasthan. Only Sia knew the effort she had put in to get a Beautician Diploma from the UK Beauty School in London. It had been totally worth it, though, when she sailed through her interview to get this job.

And her colleagues—Inder, Asha, Fern and Andy—were all excellent at their work, each one having an expertise of his own.

But meeting Ritvik had left Sia perplexed. Her focus from the age of twenty had been to be a world class beautician. But one look at the CEO of Maharaja International had turned her life topsy turvy.

With difficulty, Sia concentrated on the job at hand. She and Asha were giving a bride-to-be the works. While Asha was giving the client a foot massage, Sia was giving her a hair treatment. The other three were also busy with customers. Now wasn't the time to lose focus. She still had to prove her mettle in her new job.

Sia forcefully pushed thoughts of Ritvik away from her mind, towel-drying the bride-to-be's hair before blow drying it, even as she styled it with a hair brush. It wasn't long before she succeeded in giving her full concentration to the job at hand. Anyway, she mused, the man was way out of reach, certainly not meant for the likes of Sia.

Ritvik left Aarya in Meera's care before getting ready for work. He had a shower and dressed in a dapper, pale grey, two-piece suit teamed with an ink blue shirt and a black silk tie with motifs of the hotel emblem in rich red and gold.

Aarya clung to his legs as he thrust his feet into black leather shoes. "Sweetie pie." Ritvik lifted her into his arms to kiss her gently on her cheek. "Daddy's going to work."

"I also come."

He laughed. "Why don't we meet for lunch? I'll pick you up or send someone to get you. You want pizza, right?"

Aarya nodded, her lips drooping a bit. "'kay Daddhie."

"Don't be sad, sweetie. I love you." Ritvik pressed his lips to her forehead. "Tell you what? It's a secret."

Her eyes lit up with excitement. "Whath?" she asked in a dramatic whisper.

"Let's get a kitten or maybe two when we move to our new house next month. You know kittens are..."

"Kitthens are cath babies," yelled Aarya, jumping out of her father's arms to dance around the living room. "Shall we get two, Daddhie? Pleathe?"

"Done. But let's keep it a secret," he said, a finger on his lips, his eyes dancing with mischief. While there was no need for secrets, Aarya loved bonding with her father, as did Ritvik. "I'm leaving now." He ruffled her hair. "Will you colour that little bird in the book we got yesterday?"

"Yeth, Daddhie."

Ritvik stepped out of his suite with a smile on his face, thanking his lucky stars for blessing him with his baby girl.

He walked into the hotel's reception and forgot all about his home as he became involved in his work.

"Good morning, Ritvik," greeted Akhil Shetty, a wide smile on his face. The Front Office Manager at Maharaja International was as efficient as Vignesh Kumar, who played the same role at Rohit's Simha International in Mumbai and Ritvik was mighty chuffed with his find.

Akhil used to work under Rohit as a management trainee and had been an extremely difficult and unhappy employee. Ritvik had put in a lot of effort to improve the man's confidence and had trained him well to become what he was today. Ritvik trusted that Akhil was the right man to run his hotel on oiled wheels.

"Good morning, Akhil. How's it going?"

"Everything's in control, Ritvik. We are full today and for the next couple of weeks. And the restaurants..." Akhil brought Ritvik up-to-date on everything. "*Haan,* we have also taken on a new person to run Cleopatra's..."

"Sia Rathod." Ritvik smiled. "Yeah, I met her today morning."

Akhil laughed. "You seem omniscient."

Ritvik laughed outright even as he shrugged. "It's good if everyone thinks so," he winked. "Before I forget, I've a lunch date with my daughter at Alexander the Great at around 1.30. Aarya wants to have pizza with lots of cheese. You've got to remind me, just in case I get too involved with things here."

Akhil nodded. "Sure, Ritvik. Do you want me to bring her to you?"

"That'd be great, Akhil. Better yet, send Meghnath." Meghnath was one of the two bouncers on the premises and was built like a pillar. He also acted as bodyguard to Ritvik and his daughter when the need arose. "I have two meetings, one with accounts and the other with housekeeping. I think I should be done before lunch. At least I hope so." Ritvik waved to the front office manager before walking towards his glass enclosed cabin at one corner of the high-ceilinged reception which was right in the middle of the hotel.

The reception space used to be an open courtyard which had been enclosed on all four sides by five floors of rooms. Ritvik had added a skylight at the top and converted the courtyard into the reception of his hotel. There was a fountain right in the centre that gave the place a cool ambience. Terracotta pots of green ferns surrounded the fountain adding to the beauty of the place.

The reception was lit from floor to ceiling by wall sconces in the shape of war elephants and horses, placed strategically to enhance the royal ambience.

The heritage building used to be the summer palace of the Thakore royal family in yonder days. But their finances had dwindled over the decades and they had had to sell some of their buildings. Ritvik had purchased the manmade island in the middle of the lake along with all the buildings on it, including the royal kitchens and stables. He had transformed the main palace into his heritage hotel, keeping the royal kitchens for his personal use. One part of the stables still housed four horses, while the rest of it had been converted into a parking area. He had also added three buildings—Monarch, Sovereign and Magnate—about half a kilometre away to house the staff who didn't hail from Udaipur.

The biggest challenge had been the plumbing as he had had to install attached bathrooms to the 700-room heritage building. Without knocking down too many walls, Ritvik had adapted the smaller rooms into bathrooms. Even these were about 150-200 square feet on an average. The final tally had been four hundred rooms and suites, each one more luxurious than the other.

Ritvik walked into his cabin and gave a sigh of pleasure as he sank into his swivel chair which was placed behind an antique, well-polished desk of rosewood, with little nooks and crevices along with spacious drawers. While his paperwork was minimal due to the advent of technology, Ritvik enjoyed using the desk, along with Aarya, who especially loved the secret compartments. There were three in all. When he wasn't too busy, he encouraged Aarya to play on his desk, as they fooled around. By now, she knew how to find the stuff her father hid in the many little sections which opened only if one knew where to press.

He opened his laptop to run through his mails and replied to those which were urgent. He worked through the few papers on his in-tray when his phone pinged. It was a message from Harsh, his accounts head, reminding him about their meeting in five minutes. "On my way," replied Ritvik, getting up to shrug into his coat jacket. He took the stairs on the left side of the reception to reach the second floor and turned left to walk around the corridor in a full circle to reach the accounts department which was on the right side of the staircase. Yes, Ritvik enjoyed walking around his hotel as much as he could, simply soaking in the rich and colourful ambience. He thrived on running Maharaja International.

He met a few members of the housekeeping staff on the fifth floor about an hour later. Maria was the head of housekeeping and ruled her underlings with an iron hand in a velvet glove. "Good afternoon, Ritvik," she greeted her boss with a cup of tea.

"Good afternoon, Maria." Ritvik gave her a warm hug, bringing colour to her wrinkled face. "And thanks for the tea. It's exactly what I need." He waved to Chitra and Som, both Maria's immediate assistants, pointing to the chairs. "Sit down, guys. Now tell me." He listened to all their reports and a couple of requests patiently. "So, you want me to hire five more hands?" When Maria nodded, he said, "Let me talk to Akhil. I'm sure it shouldn't be a problem. Maria, why don't you do something? Do send word around to the rest of your colleagues asking them if they have any family members or friends who need a job. We would save a lot of time and effort that way. Works?"

"That's perfect, Ritvik. Which was exactly what I was going to ask you next. Rita has a younger brother who has just completed his tenth standard exams. She asked me if he could get a job here."

Ritvik nodded. "Of course, Maria, as long as he has turned eighteen. Ask the boy to send an application through Rita. You can hand it over to Harsh. I'll ask Akhil to take care of it. It's the same with all the staff. Their family members get first option for jobs here. Got that?" When all three nodded with a smile, Ritvik stood up, indicating that the meeting was over. Looking at his silver watch, he waved to them, wishing them a good day, and rushed out as it was almost time for his lunch date with Aarya.

4

It was ten days since Sia had joined Cleopatra's and she had the salon running exceptionally well when Dayanita Thakore walked in without an appointment. "Who's there? I need the works," she called out imperiously.

"Good afternoon, ma'am," responded Sia in a soft voice as she blow-dried her client's hair. "Please have a seat. Someone will be with you as soon as possible."

"You are new," declared Dayanita, eyeing Sia snootily, "and obviously don't know who I am. Get someone to attend to me immediately."

Sia smiled at her client—Rakshita—through the mirror, saying, "I hope you like your new hair style, ma'am. Here you go." She brought a mirror to hold it behind Rakshita's head, showing her the stylish cut.

"Bitch!" Dayanita snarled. "Fern, Andyyyyy," she screamed, stamping her right foot in a fine temper.

"They're busy with clients, ma'am. You'll need to excuse all of us. Let me check when someone would be free to attend to you." Sia walked to the counter to print a bill for her client, even as she spoke to Dayanita Thakore.

"How dare you? You obviously don't know who I am. I…"

"That's right, ma'am," Sia said calmly, looking the woman deeply in her eye. "You'll obviously tell me at your convenience."

Dayanita walked speedily to Sia; her hand raised as if to slap her. "I'll…"

"…calm down first," said Sia, holding the other woman's wrist firmly. She smiled gently, continuing, "Are you royalty by any chance? The last time I heard, India had become a republic in 1950. I hope you're aware that I'm not your slave."

"I'll report you to your CEO right now, you bloody bitch. I'll make sure you're thrown out of your job right this very minute. You don't know me." Dayanita did a right about turn and fumed out of the salon.

Sia wiped the grin from her face with difficulty as she handed the bill to Rakshita.

"Don't you know that the lady is Dayanita Thakore?" Rakshita asked. "She's a princess. Her family used to own this palace before it became Maharaja International." She continued in a low voice, "And she can be trouble with a capital T."

"Thank you for the heads up, ma'am," said Sia dispassionately. "I'm running an efficient salon. We can't drop our clients in the middle of a service to attend to anyone for whatever reason."

Rakshita nodded, a smile on her face. The new salon manager was not just an excellent hairstylist, it seemed. It looked like she was also a woman of grit.

"I hope you're going to be here for a long time for my sake though. I love my new style."

"Thank you, ma'am," said Sia, swiping the client's debit card before handing her the customer copy of the transaction. "Have a good day."

Dayanita barged into the CEO's cabin, in a roaring temper. She had never felt so insulted. That woman must go, *today*. Ritvik had to listen to her.

Akhil got up from the visitor's chair the moment he saw Dayanita Thakore walk in. He knew for a fact that no more work would get done, not until the princess left the premises. "I'll get on with my work, Ritvik. I'll be seeing you around. *Haan*, one more thing. You need to take Aarya for an injection. Your appointment with the paediatrician is in forty-five minutes." Akhil gave his boss a wink from behind Dayanita's back before leaving the cabin, shutting the door softly behind him.

"Ritvik!" Dayanita's voice was shaking with temper as she screeched his name. She would have loved to jump into his arms, but she knew that he was capable of sliding out of her embrace. She needed to wear him down slowly and steadily. She had been working on it over the past two years. Well, twenty-year-old Dayanita was in no hurry to get married, though her grandmother Santhini Devi Thakore was keen for her to tie the knot with Ritvik Bansal. He was the man with the money who also owned their main palace these days, making him perfect son-in-law material for the cash-starved royal household.

Ritvik looked up from his phone after he sent a WhatsApp message to Akhil which read, "You ditcher, I'll get you for this," followed by a laughter emoticon.

"Sit down Nita. How have you been?" In Ritvik's opinion, she was a royal—pun intended—pain in the ass. But he had his reasons for keeping her happy, though he drew the line at being touched. While she obviously believed—of course Ritvik knew all about it—that she was training him for the role of her future husband, he had coached her to keep her distance. Her touch was creepy and he always ensured that there was at least a couple of feet distance between them.

"I was feeling awesome until the moment I entered your hotel's salon, Ritvik," declared Dayanita dramatically, sitting down on a chair with a thud. She waited for him to ask her why but gave up after a few minutes when he refused to lift his head from his laptop. "Aren't you going to ask me why?" Her words were a tempestuous scream now.

"I'm sure you're going to tell me, Nita." Ritvik refused to look up as he spoke to her. "Oh, would you like some coffee? I'm going to order some for me." Otherwise, he wouldn't have bothered to stand on ceremony with her.

Flames leaped out of Dayanita's eyes as she gritted her teeth. It was so difficult not to scream at the man. He drove her up the wall. Here she was, a beautiful specimen of womanhood, and the man was completely unaware of her. Any red-blooded man would desire her. Was Ritvik's libido not up to mark? Dayanita had her doubts. No, she refused to accept he was gay, though some of her friends had suggested that. Why would he have a surrogate child otherwise? With difficulty, Dayanita pulled her rambling thoughts together to get to the matter at hand. "Yeah, I'll have fresh strawberry milkshake. Coffee is bad for my complexion," she tittered, giving him a corner-eyed glance to see if he was checking out the said complexion. Her temper rose again when she realised that Ritvik was still focussed on his laptop, even though he lifted the phone to place the order. "And the reason I am disturbing you at work is that... that woman at Cleopatra's, she..."

"I'm sure she has a name," said Ritvik, mild sarcasm in his voice, still not looking at his unwanted guest.

"Ritvik, listen to me." Dayanita's voice was demanding. She got angrier when a waiter knocked on the door and brought in Ritvik's coffee and her milkshake. "She needs to go. I insist."

"What?" Ritvik finally turned to give her his full attention, only because he had begun to sip from his coffee. "What, or rather, whom are you talking about?" he asked, his right eyebrow raised in query.

Dayanita stared at the man in front of her, pursing her lips tightly to stop the drool from flowing out. He looked amazingly handsome; way more royal than either of her brothers. She would kill to get married to him and she didn't really give a damn that he didn't show much interest in her. Over the past two years, in her pursuit of him, Dayanita had arrived at the bizarre conclusion that Ritvik Bansal was shy of women. It was up to her to bring him out of his shell. Getting her wool-gathering thoughts together once again, she said impatiently, "I'm talking about the new recruit at Cleopatra's. She has to go."

"May I know why?" It took Ritvik a couple of seconds to realise that Dayanita was talking about Sia.

"She's bad for our hotel's reputation."

Ignoring the 'our' for the time being, Ritvik asked, "She is? How?"

"She treated me—a regular client—with total disrespect. She..."

"Are you talking about Sia Rathod?" he asked, relishing his coffee despite the pesky guest who had thrust herself upon him. Dayanita liked to believe that she had ownership over Maharaja International just because the palace used to belong to her family once upon a time. She conveniently forgot that Ritvik had paid them one crore rupees more than the market value, only because the whole family had kept whining about their lack of finances.

"If that's her name." Dayanita scowled heavily as she took a sip of the milkshake.

"Isn't the milkshake to your taste?" he asked, tongue tucked firmly in cheek, a glimmer of amusement in his charcoal gaze. Dayanita was classically beautiful, though her expression was another matter altogether. Her patrician nose was always wrinkled as if she could smell dirt, resembling her grandmother, both in looks and expression.

"What? Oh, you mean the milkshake. It's perfect, Ritvik, just as everything else in this hotel. But then, I always knew that you demand and receive the best. That's the reason I know you'll agree with me that this woman should be dismissed. I think..."

Ritvik raised a hand to stop her from speaking further. "You still haven't told me why."

"Ritvik." Dayanita pouted at him, obviously believing that she looked cute. But Ritvik refused to pay any attention as he poured himself a second cup of coffee and continued to savour it, waiting for her to tell him why she wanted Sia to go. Not that he gave a damn about Dayanita's opinion. "She insulted me."

"Is that so? What did she do?" His voice was mild, as was his expression.

"She told me... imagine, she had the gall to tell me there was no one free to attend to me. She insisted that I would have to wait. I, Dayanita Thakore of the Thakore Royals! How dare she? When I asked her if she knew who I was, she... she..." Dayanita appeared to choke on her milkshake as she placed her glass on Ritvik's desk before covering her face with both her hands. She didn't notice him noticing her watching him through the gaps between her fingers, as she pretended to cry. When she realised that he was on the verge of turning back to his laptop, Dayanita removed her hands in a hurry and said, "She dared to tell me that even if I was royalty, the country had become a republic in 1950 and she wasn't anyone's slave."

Ritvik burst out laughing, adding fuel to Dayanita's already boiling temper. His massive shoulders shook with mirth as he continued to laugh till tears poured down his cheeks.

"I can't see what's funny," Dayanita snarled, pushing her chair back noisily to stand up. She didn't know who she wanted to kill first—the woman at Cleopatra's or Ritvik Bansal.

Ritvik stopped laughing, wiping his eyes with a tissue. "Hey, no offense. If Sia said that to you she really needs to be pulled up. She can't treat customers this way. Let me talk to her about it."

"Do that. You'll know that she needs to be dismissed. I'm going off now. I'm in no mood to have a facial or pedicure, not after the way I have been treated. But I'll come back tomorrow maybe. Do make sure she's not working at Cleopatra's by then."

No please; no sorry. Some royalty she was. "Are you sure you wouldn't like to join Aarya and me for lunch?" Ritivk asked, confident that she'd refuse his invitation, knowing how the young lady abhorred children.

Dayanita had a tough time holding back the shudder which threatened to shake her body. She so hated kids. No way was she going to spend time with Ritvik's spoilt brat. "Not today Ritvik. I need to go. Mamma's expecting me home as we're having some guests over."

Ritvik nodded, watching her go before lifting the phone to call the salon. "Hello Andy. This is Ritvik. Is Sia free?" When Andy answered in the affirmative, Ritvik left instructions for Sia to meet him in his office immediately.

"Sia," Andy went to his new boss. "Ritvik would like to meet you in his office."

"Oh God!" Sia shut her eyes tightly before opening them. "I hope I haven't landed myself in a soup."

"You shouldn't worry, Sia," said Fern. All her new colleagues knew about Dayanita's drama of the morning and were all admiration for the way Sia had handled the situation.

Sia looked at Fern with a frown on her smooth forehead. "I'm not sure. The lady did threaten to go to the CEO. And now the man's summoned me to his cabin. Tch! Just now when I'm settling into the job so well too." More than anything, Sia wished that she had slapped the other woman hard. At least then she wouldn't have minded losing her job so much. Removing her apron, she brushed back her hair and touched up her lips with a nude gloss before stepping out of the salon followed by a chorus of 'good luck' wishes from the others.

She stepped into the CEO's cabin after knocking. "Good afternoon, sir." Sia stood in front of Ritvik's desk, eyeing him warily.

"Sit down, Sia," said Ritvik, shutting his laptop. "So how are you settling down?" he asked, giving her a smile, which made her heart do a jig.

An answering smile lit up her face as Sia did his bidding and sat on the chair recently vacated by Dayanita. "Very well, sir."

"You should call me Ritvik."

Sia nodded. "Thank you Ritvik."

"So! I heard that you had a strange customer today. Do you want to talk about it?"

Sia saw that he was still smiling and didn't seem angry at all. Could the woman's threats have all been empty? Some of the tension left her body as she sat up straight. "I suppose you're talking about Dayanita Thakore's visit?" When Ritvik nodded, Sia continued, "The lady hadn't called us for an appointment. All of us were busy when she arrived. I asked her to wait and," Sia shrugged, "She didn't take it well. I..."

"I don't think it really was as simple as you put it." Ritvik sat back in his chair, a fist under his chin, a trace of amusement in his black-as-sin eyes.

"No, it wasn't. Ms Thakore raised her hand to hit me." Sia held his gaze boldly. "I won't apologise for blocking her, Ritvik. I held her wrist firmly and stopped her. She asked me if I knew who she was. I told her that even if she was royalty..."

"...India had become a republic and you were no one's slave." Ritvik grinned. "I must congratulate you, Sia. I am proud you're on my team. I know that the customer is king, but I draw the line when people take my employees for granted. Kudos!" He got up from his chair. "I just wanted to check if Ms Thakore had rattled your confidence. I see that I needn't have worried." He walked forward to pat her on her shoulder. "I'm hearing all good about Cleopatra's nowadays, run by your capable hands. Keep up the great work!"

Sia had also got up now and couldn't stop the colour from flaring up her cheeks with all that praise going straight to her head. And his touch on her shoulder had given her heart palpitations. Sia felt a tightening of her breasts while her wretched nipples perked up. She turned sideways, not wanting Ritvik to see her body's response to his touch. "Thank you again Ritvik." Her voice came out in a hoarse whisper as her throat felt choked due to an increase in her pulse rate.

Feeling too awkward to look up at him, Sia didn't realise that her new boss had, in fact, noticed her body's response to his touch.

ayanita was disgusted with Ritvik Bansal, Maharaja International, Cleopatra's and that new woman running the salon—in that order. She got into the luxurious sedan that her family could ill afford and roared out of the compound of the 5-star hotel, speeding towards her home which was about fifteen minutes away.

She burned with envy every time she visited the hotel, but she couldn't help herself. The heritage palace used to belong to her family, the Thakores. Just because Ritvik Bansal had the money, how could he just usurp them of the palace which had been built by her ancestors, way back in 1580? How could someone wipe away four hundred and thirty-seven years of history in one sweep?

Dayanita's father Gajendar Thakore had taken over the farming of lands from his father. First drought and then floods had put paid to the crops over the last ten years. Then there were the exorbitant expenses which the family incurred while running the royal household. Her grandmother Santhini Devi liked to believe that they were the rulers of the area even today. While the two palaces had become faded over the past few decades, she continued to keep an army of servants to take care of both. That, along with the luxurious living, extravagant entertaining and exotic travel had become too much of a financial burden for Gajendar to handle.

Things had come to a head when Gajendar realised that there was no money to give his three children the expensive higher education which they deserved, after having done so well at school. The loans had mounted with his mother insisting that not one square foot of land of theirs should be sold. After thinking long and hard, Gajendar had arrived at the conclusion that the palace on the island had to be sold along with the land surrounding it. Only that would get them out of all the loans and also pave the way for the future generation. That place used to be the summer palace of the Thakores in yonder days. It was kept locked up most of the months, only thrown open to lavish entertainment during the summer. This activity had simply added to his monetary woes.

When the Bansals had come for a stay at the palace, introduced via common friends, Gajendar had mentioned that he was considering the idea of selling the palace. It had been a vague thought at the back of his mind and he happened to mention it after a few drinks. He had been surprised when Ritvik Bansal had come back with an offer the very next month. All hell had broken loose when he mentioned this to his mother. But Gajendar was a desperate man. Finally, he had threatened to commit suicide to convince his mother to let him sell the palace. And that's how it had gone into Ritvik's hands four years ago, later to become Maharaja International.

Dayanita didn't really notice the ornate gates to her home which were opened the moment the security guard noticed her car from far away. Nor did she bother to acknowledge his salute as she drove down the long drive, her angry eyes fixed on the building which was her home. Yes, the structure was still strong, but barely so. All the money which had come from the sale of the heritage property had gone to pay back humongous loans along with hefty interests and her brothers' education as both Indrajeet and Rajvardhan had chosen to go to the Harvard Business School in Boston. While her father had encouraged her to study abroad too, Dayanita had refused, thanks to her grandmother's advice. She had settled for a degree in English literature from a local college.

Gajendar had refused to spend money on renovating their home, despite all the tantrums thrown by both, his mother and his daughter. His wife Ragini was quiet and tried her best to please everyone—her husband, her mother-in-law and her children. He had been clear that he didn't want to blow up all the money since their only source of income was from farming which was erratic at best. It would be a few years before his sons started earning an income and the lavish household needed to be maintained in style until then. And then there was Dayanita's wedding to be performed.

Just now, Dayanita walked into her home and shuddered as she couldn't help comparing the faded silk upholstery and dull velvet curtains to those at Maharaja International. The furniture was also sparse. They could do with a few more sofas and divans. Why the fuck couldn't she have the luxurious life she craved?

"Maa," she called out imperiously as she walked the length of the marble floor of the main hall which was about four thousand square feet in area. Her mother must be in the kitchen, supervising lunch. Dayanita shuddered! How boring. It was her grandmother she connected with more than her mother. She suddenly turned left, towards Santhini Devi's quarters. "Grandma." Santhini Devi was still attached to the British era and insisted that her grandchildren addressed her as Grandma instead of *Daadima*, which was too low class, according to her.

"Hello my dear. Come and sit down. How was your morning? Did you meet Ritvik?" It was Santhini Devi's idea that Dayanita should wed the 5-star hotel owner. As for Dayanita's mother Ragini, she had simply nodded her head when the matriarch had suggested it to her granddaughter. This was also the reason why the old lady had refused permission to send Dayanita abroad for further studies.

"Oh Grandma, I hate the man. He's such an idiot. And you know what? I hate children. He keeps bringing Aarya into every conversation. Why the hell can't he take me out for a meal, just the two of us? Can you imagine that he asked me to go to lunch along with him and that grubby brat of his? I'm fed up." The words came tumbling out as Dayanita poured her frustration to her grandmother.

Santhini Devi nodded, her wicked eyes admiring her granddaughter's classical beauty. "I know you don't like children, my darling. But I hope you didn't exactly tell Ritvik that."

Dayanita grimaced. "Not really. I remember your advice only too well. I just told him that we're having guests at home and escaped. And listen, there's more. You know what happened...?" Dayanita went on to tell her grandmother about her encounter with Sia and how Ritvik had laughed at her insults. "I don't think I want to marry him. He..."

"Don't be silly, Dayanita. Have you forgotten that he's a billionaire many times over? You'd be a fool to let go of him. And listen, I'll have to teach you how to deal with men. They don't like to be ordered around."

Dayanita looked at her grandmother strangely, curbing her irritation with difficulty. This same woman ruled the Thakore household with a rod of iron and ordered her father about all the time. It was from her that Dayanita had learned the art of being a perfect shrew. And now she said that men didn't like to be ordered around. Talk about giving out confusing vibes!

"But Grandma, you give instructions to Pappa all the time." Dayanita pouted, jumping to her feet and walking around the room restlessly.

"That's because he is my son. Moreover, your father is too simple. He lacks cunning and needs to be guided forcefully. Otherwise, he would let go of everything that your ancestors have worked so hard to bring together under the family umbrella."

That made sense. Look at how her father had sold away their summer palace. Santhini Devi had told Dayanita a lot of stories about their brave forefathers who had won over the land from wars fought so bravely. "You're right, Grandma."

"Your son has arrived, Mamma, and lunch is served. Why don't the two of you come over to the dining room?" Ragini stood outside the doorway when she asked the question. She was too scared of her autocratic mother-in-law and did her best to keep her distance.

"You go and see that everything's in place. We'll join you in a few minutes," said Santhini Devi imperiously, her face unsmiling. What had her son seen in this mouse who he had insisted on marrying her? She conveniently forgot that it was she who had tried to force the match on her son as Ragini had come with a hefty dowry. What she hadn't expected was for her son to fall in love with the mouse. Santhini Devi felt that Gajendar was a slave to his wife and she simply couldn't tolerate that.

"So, what do you think I should do?" asked Dayanita, thoroughly perplexed.

"You shouldn't try to tell Ritvik how to run his hotel, whom to hire and whom to dismiss. If that woman insulted you, there are other ways to deal with the issue. What did you say her name was?"

"Sia Rathod." Dayanita's lips were drooping with dissatisfaction as she frowned at her grandmother.

"Let's have lunch first and then we'll get our heads together on how to deal with this Rathod woman, shall we?"

The frown disappeared from Dayanita's face and she gave Santhini Devi a wide grin. "Now you're talking, Grandma. Let's go. I'm famished."

6

itvik had an early dinner with Aarya that evening. The little chatterbox was rather quiet as she drank the chicken soup with a small spoon. The immunisation injection for Hepatitis A which the paediatrician had given Aarya had made her weak and consequently quiet. Ritvik checked to see if she had a temperature; she did, but thankfully it wasn't very high.

Ritvik looked at his daughter's pinched little face, wishing that he could take some of her pain. "Does it hurt a lot, baby?"

She leaned her head against his arm, obviously exhausted. "Yeth, Daddhie." She shifted into his lap, cuddling against his stomach, her thumb tucked into her mouth.

Ritvik waited for Aarya to fall asleep before getting up and settling down on the recliner in the living room, snuggling her little body close against his chest, keeping her warm. It was barely 8.30 pm when the duo fell fast asleep.

Meera switched off the doorbell and settled back in her room in front of the TV, keeping the volume low and her door slightly ajar just in case either of them called out to her.

Meera was from Mahabaleshwar and had always taken care of children. Unmarried, she had no kids of her own, but treated all her wards with love and care. She had known the Bansals for many years during her stint at taking care of their neighbours' children. She had been looking for a job when Ritvik had called her a few weeks before Aarya was born. He had promised her a job and sent her tickets on a luxury bus from Mahabaleshwar to Mumbai and a flight to Udaipur, without telling her what the job was. Knowing the youngest Bansal son from his infancy, Meera hadn't hesitated before giving an affirmative answer. While all the three Bansal siblings were affectionate, Ritvik had always been her favourite. Even while being mischievous, he had a streak of compassion which touched Meera's heart. So she had caught the bus, then the subsequent flight and here she was, working with Ritvik Bansal since a few months over two years. It had been worth the effort, since Aarya was a darling child. She only wished—she knew not by what right—that Ritvik would provide the little girl with a mother. An inadvertent sigh overtook Meera before she could stop it. She continued to watch her favourite TV serial, not really surprised when her services weren't called upon until she went to bed at 11 pm. Ritvik was a hands-on father, always there for his daughter, making Meera feel like a fraud at times for taking a salary for her job. But then, he became busy at times, and that's when she felt her services were really useful. Then again, at no time had either Ritvik or Aarya treated her like an employee. Meera always felt as if she was part of the family.

It wasn't really a surprise when Ritvik woke up at 6.30 am with a crick in his neck. But the gentle weight in his arms made him almost forget his pain. He brushed back the curls which had tumbled over Aarya's face with tenderness, glad to find that she had no fever.

Aarya opened her eyes and gave him a toothy grin. "Gu mornin' Daddhie." She sat up on his stomach to rub her eyes. "You are my bedh," she gurgled with laughter.

"Good morning, my little imp. Oh yeah!" He laughed, before lifting her up in his arms to carry her over to the bathroom. "I love you, sweetie."

Aarya threw both her arms around his neck, giving him a wet kiss on his cheek. "I love you, Daddhie."

Ritvik left Aarya in Meera's care before taking a shower. The pain in his neck refused to go and that was when he struck upon a plan. He couldn't help but recall the memory of Sia's lush breasts thrusting against her white shirt, the nipples having gone pebble hard when he touched her shoulder. He would go to Cleopatra's and have a head massage. He pulled on a pair of Bermuda shorts and a button down half shirt, before thrusting his feet into leather sandals.

"Meera Aunty, I need to go out for a while. Please give Aarya her breakfast." He turned to his daughter and said, "Daddy needs to go somewhere, sweetie.

You have breakfast with aunty. I'll be back in some time. We both will have lunch together."

"'kay Daddhie. I'm goin' to see carthoon."

"Right sweetie. You do that." Ritvik ruffled her hair before kissing Aarya on the top of her head. Waving to both of them, he left to rush down three flights of stairs before walking to the back of the hotel where Cleopatra's was. He entered to find Inder and Fern who hailed him exuberantly. "Hey, good morning," he responded to them with equal enthusiasm. "Where are the others?"

"Andy is giving a client a massage and Asha is with another client for a manicure-pedicure," Inder answered. "What can I do for you, Ritvik?"

"Where's Sia?"

"Were you looking for me?" Sia came out of the bathroom where she had gone to change into her work attire. Seeing Ritvik, she greeted him with a smile, "Good morning, boss." It was difficult holding on to her smile when she ran her eyes over him. The first time she met him, Ritvik had been dressed casually in jeans and a t-shirt. Yesterday, he had been in a formal suit when she met him in his cabin. Today, in shorts and a casual shirt, he was breathtaking. It was a wonder that she was still breathing after catching an eyeful of him first thing in the morning. Sia pressed a hand against her chest, trying to calm down her pounding heart. It was with great difficulty that she focussed on what he was saying.

"Morning, Sia. I need a head massage, desperately. Are you free to give me one?"

"Of course! Would you like to settle down in that cabin?" Sia pointed to the one on the far left. "I'll be with you in two minutes."

Ritvik settled down in the comfortable salon chair, his feet stretched out on the ottoman. He turned his neck this way and that, unable to find a suitable position as it continued to hurt.

Sia walked in, pushing a trolley which held steaming aromatic oil, combs and towels, to see him turning restlessly in his chair. "Is something wrong?"

"I've sprained my neck. It hurts like a bitch," he bit out.

"The massage will definitely help. But I'll get you an icepack first. Can you please take off your shirt?" Sia fled even as she noticed his hands moving towards the shirt buttons through the mirror. Wondering how she was going to survive the next hour, Sia removed a frozen pack from the freezer and went back to the cabin. She dropped the pack on the trolley, her pulse going haywire when her eyes encountered his amazing chest in the mirror. Luckily for her, his eyes were shut, thick and long lashes resting against his manly cheeks. She took some moments to study his bronzed, muscular shoulders and chest which tapered into a lean waist. His chest was liberally sprinkled with curly hair, just enough to make a woman want to swoon into his arms. Feeling like a voyeur, Sia turned her head away to remove a large, fluffy towel to spread it over his chest. She lifted his open hair and piled it into a loose knot on the top of his head. "Can you tell me where exactly it hurts?"

When Ritvik pointed to the left side of his neck without opening his eyes, Sia said in warning, "I'm going to press an icepack to that spot," before placing it gently against the area and holding it there.

Ritvik gave a long and deep groan. "Thanks, Sia. That feels so good."

Sia smiled, looking at him in the mirror. Gaining confidence as his eyes continued to remain shut, her silvery grey eyes ran over his body boldly. His broad feet were bare as they rested on the ottoman, as were his long, long legs. His khaki shorts covered him from hip to knee. Her eyes paused at his washboard abs which the towel hadn't quite managed to cover. She dragged her gaze away with an effort to concentrate on his neck as she lifted the icepack and turned it over before pressing the other side down over the troubled spot, satisfied to hear Ritvik's groan of pleasure.

After some time, she removed the ice pack before pouring the fragrant oil in her left palm. Rubbing it between her hands, Sia set out to massage Ritvik's shoulders, working towards his neck, while he continued to remain silent, his eyes shut. She could see that his breathing was even as his chest rose and fell rhythmically under the towel.

Her palms and fingers tingled as she rubbed them firmly over his shoulders, revelling in the sensation. He was all hard muscle and sinew, not one little bit of spare flesh. His skin was bronzed to an even golden brown. Sia was hard pressed to refrain from kissing the pulse beating steadily at the side of his neck. She worked dexterously with her hands despite the lusty thoughts which scampered through her mind, orchestrated by her hammering heart.

Ritvik groaned, opening his slumberous gaze to look at her through the mirror when she pressed a thumb to the damaged spot. "That's the spot. Go easy on it, please."

She gave him a nod and a weak smile, her grey eyes glowing silver as she tenderly stroked the spot upwards, keen to relieve his pain.

"Oh yes! That feel so good," moaned Ritvik, shutting his eyes again, giving himself up to her ministrations. He almost went to sleep as Sia opened the loose knot of his long hair and oiled it. She pulled and stroked and massaged every inch of his scalp, working her way towards his neck once again, downwards this time. After forty-five minutes of kneading his head and neck, Sia set up a hair steamer above Ritvik's head and switched it on. She also brought a hot towel for his neck. After the excess oil was removed from his neck, she applied a hot water bag, holding it in place over the left side of his neck.

Though Ritvik's eyes were closed, he was completely awake as he underwent the treatment. He had caught the tinge of colour on Sia's cheeks and had kept his eyelids firmly shut, not to cause her any further embarrassment. Sia was good with her hands while her touch on his head, neck and shoulders had aroused him. The first time he saw her, he had noticed her in passing just as any other red-blooded man would have. She was attractive and was also good at her job.

But yesterday was the first time Ritvik had really taken notice. It wasn't everybody who could stand up to Dayanita Thakore. That woman wore her shroud of royalty like a weapon and people who came in contact rarely had the guts to speak to her, let alone cross swords. He had been impressed by the way Sia had dealt with Dayanita. Attractive, efficient and bold! Sia seemed to be a lethal combo. Ritvik wanted to know her more. It had been at least three years since Ritvik had felt a spark of attraction towards a woman. There was a time when Rohit had teased him *ad nauseam* of being a ladykiller and his elder brother had spoken the truth after all. That had been one phase of Ritvik's life. Later, after being chased by women only because of his looks and money—none of them seemed to care that there was an intelligent mind lurking behind his hot looks—Ritvik had arrived at the decision that he never wanted a permanent relationship with one. That was also the time when he decided to become a single father. When his baby was growing in some stranger's womb, Ritvik wasn't in a mental state to have an affair. When Aarya was born, he gave her all his attention. Between his busy career as a hotelier and being a single parent to his little girl, Ritvik didn't make time for women. Yes, he was aware that he could have made the time if he had really set his mind to it. But it was just that he hadn't felt the need.

Right now, though, it looked like Sia had woken up the sleeping man in him. Ritvik opened his eyes and stretched after she moved the steamer and hot water bag away. "Sia..." His charcoal eyes delved deeply into her smoky grey gaze through the mirror. "That was simply amazing! My neck," he turned his head, first to the left and then to the right before continuing, "is as good as new." He smiled at her before getting up from his chair, the towel falling off his magnificent chest and making Sia's eyes stretch wide. Ritvik's smile grew wider when he saw what had caught her attention. Removing his shirt from the hanger, he shrugged his wide shoulders into it. "Thank you so much. Tell you what!" He paused as if to wonder if she was really hearing his words as her expression continued to remain dazed.

"What?" Sia lifted her gaze from his chest—it was covered now anyway—up to his eyes as she asked the question.

"Have dinner with me."

"I..." Her right hand went to her throat as if that would bring down the wild beating of her pulse. "Er..."

"I promise to behave." He gave her a cheeky grin, his left eye closing in a wink.

Hot colour bloomed in Sia's cheeks as a smile broke out on her face. "Okay, boss."

"That's my girl. I'll pick you up from the staff quarters at seven. Casual should be fine."

"Can we make that eight? I'll be finishing here only after seven."

"Done." He showed her a thumbs-up before stepping into his sandals.

"I need to wash your hair."

"That's fine, Sia. I'll do it. I need a shower anyway. I'll see you in the evening." He left.

Sia sat back in the chair he had vacated with a thud. Whoosh! It felt as if she had stepped out of the centre of a tornado. The man was a livewire, emitting such energy, even with his eyes closed. She wondered how her heart was going to survive a dinner date with him.

Sia grinned suddenly. What the hell! She looked forward to an evening out with Ritvik Bansal.

I n a way, Ritvik was glad that he could sit with Aarya
while she had her dinner before leaving for his date
with Sia. She insisted on feeding pieces of chicken
to her father as she munched on the *biryani* which
Meera had prepared, spooning the *boondi raita* into
her little mouth in between. "Some more, Daddhie?"
Aarya tilted her head to one side as she did her best to
persuade her father to eat more.

Ritvik shook his head. "No more for me, little one.
I'm off to have a full dinner. I'll grow fat." He winked
at her.

Aarya gurgled with laughter. "Daddhie go fat."

"Very funny!" Ritvik tweaked her nose. He got up
when she finished eating to lift her into his arms. "I'm
off, sweetie. You be a good girl and go to sleep before
ten. I'll see you in the morning." He kissed her on her
forehead, wishing her good night.

"Gu nigthe Daddhie." Aarya kissed her father's
cheek before jumping out of his arms. "I'm going to
play. Bye."

Sia had just stepped down from her second-floor
studio apartment in Monarch when she saw the

vintage car chugging into the compound of the staff quarters. She couldn't stop from smiling widely at the cute Ford Convertible which was painted a bright red. It appeared so cheerful

Ritvik stopped the car right next to her and gave her a grin as he got out. "Do you like it? Doesn't it remind you of Archie's old jalopy?" He seemed like a kid with a toy.

"Eh? I don't know what a jalopy is." Sia looked blank. "It looks cute, however," she said, though her eyes were studying him. He was wearing dark blue jeans and a white linen shirt, the sight of the clothes and the man in them making her heart do some quick somersaults.

Ritvik gave a mental shrug. So, what if she wasn't familiar with Archie comics? "As do you," he said in return, eyeing her from the top of her head to the tips of her toes. Sia was also in jeans but the similarity in their outfits ended there. Her voluptuous body appeared sexy in the stretch jeans which followed the shape of her legs faithfully. She wore a brilliant red lacy top over a camisole of the same shade, her narrow feet encased in red stilettos, again in the exact same shade. Her hair was loose while her face was made up minimally, with mascara and lipstick. Ritvik wondered how she would taste. Pushing the thought away, he took her hand in his, guiding her to the passenger side of the car. "I hope you like chicken."

Sia was dazed, a blush on her cheeks. Had he just said that she looked cute? Before she could absorb that, he had taken her hand in his, making her pulse skitter, causing her mind to go blank. Sia sat in the car, looking up at him, her expression questioning. "You said something?"

Ritvik looked at her through the car window, his dark eyes glowing. It had been such a long time since he had been struck by such a powerful attraction. "Do you like chicken?"

Sia nodded. "Yes."

"Great. Let's go." He walked around to get into the driver's seat.

Suddenly, Sia felt the space in the car shrinking. Actually, with the windows open and the seats separated, there was a lot of room. But being with Ritvik in close quarters, it was really difficult for Sia to deal with her body's reaction. She moved as far away from him as possible, sticking to the door.

"Are you comfortable?" asked Ritvik, gunning the engine.

"Yeah, thanks."

He took off at a comfortable pace, the car being able to speed at a maximum of forty kmph, leaving the island to cross the bridge into the city. He drove steadily for about an hour through heavy traffic, chatting desultorily about nothing in particular before they reached Hotel Jaiwana Haveli in Chandpole.

"I've heard a lot about the rooftop restaurant here with an awesome view, though I've never been here before. Have you?" Ritvik asked Sia as they walked up the stairs side by side, all the way up to the fourth floor.

Sia answered him without looking at him, as she pretended to concentrate on the steps, while the truth was that she was totally aware of Ritvik, her breathing having gone haywire. "No. I haven't been around Udaipur yet."

Ritvik nodded, making a mental note of that. If he had his way, he would be the one to show Sia around Udaipur, the heritage city he had fallen in love with. They reached the rooftop restaurant and he chose the table which was in a corner from where they could watch Lake Pichola and the buildings surrounding it.

They went through the menu before Sia asked for a glass of fresh orange juice. Ritvik gave her order to the waiter before requesting a fresh lime soda for himself along with some *veg pakoras*, promising to order the mains some time later. "So, where are you from, Sia?" asked Ritvik, relaxing back in his chair.

"Have you heard of Dholpur? It's to the north east of Rajasthan and a night's journey by train from Udaipur. I was born and brought up there."

"Dholpur reeks of history I think." When she nodded, he continued, "From Dholpur to Delhi to London to Udaipur must have been one interesting journey." His voice invited her to tell him more.

Sia's smile didn't reach her eyes this time as she popped a peanut into her mouth. There was one more town which was missing from her CV—Jhunjhunu. But she didn't plan to talk about it, not to Ritvik, or anyone else for that matter. "You can say that. I suppose I have always wanted more out of life than the mundane." She grimaced as she recalled her life some years ago. Sia gave herself a mental shake, refusing to delve on those memories. The therapy had worked wonders in healing her soul. She wasn't in touch with her family nowadays, not even aware if her father was alive or dead.

"And you managed to achieve that." It wasn't a question. Her CV—yes, Ritvik had gone back to check it yesterday—had said it all about how she had managed to do a beautician's course in London what with her small-town background and tenth standard education.

"It wasn't easy, but I'm determined like that." Sia grinned, feeling proud of how she had shaped her life. "And you? You're from Mumbai, right?"

Ritvik shook his head. "From Mahabaleshwar, actually. It's a hill station about six hours away from Mumbai."

Sia looked at him wide-eyed. He seemed all slick and city bred. She'd have to check more about Mahabaleshwar. She had never heard of the place. "How come you set up a hotel here in Udaipur?"

"Being from a hotelier family, I've never thought of doing anything else. I fell in love with the heritage palace during a family holiday here. We were lucky enough to have a chance to see the palace when a close friend introduced us to the Thakore family." He laughed when Sia grimaced. "Oh yeah, I'm talking about Dayanita Thakore's parents. I garnered that they were keen to sell the property as they were strapped for cash. The rest, as they say, is history and here I am, enjoying running Maharaja International to my heart's content."

He made it all sound so simple. But he must have obviously worked really hard to be where he was. Sia didn't miss the intelligence which shone out of Ritvik's eyes. That's what made him all the more attractive to her.

Sia spoke of her life in Delhi where she had worked at three different beauty salons, being paid a pittance which had barely helped her make ends meet. She glossed over her struggles though it wasn't very difficult for Ritvik to read between the lines. He couldn't help but admire the woman's grit, having reached where she had by sheer dint of hard work and determination.

Ritvik, in turn, spoke of his parents, his siblings and their hotels. Sia listened, fascinated. She realised that he was the baby of the family. They must have definitely spoilt him. But that had obviously not stopped him from carving a niche for himself.

They ate their way through the *pakoras* before ordering *butter chicken, tandoori rotis, moong ki dal* and *jeera rice* along with *kachumber*.

They sat back for some time after the food was eaten as Ritvik pointed out the City Palace and other sights to Sia.

"There's something about all this water which I find absolutely fascinating," Sia remarked. "There seems to be a lake whichever way you turn."

"I agree. That's one of the main reasons why I was keen to get my hands on the property where the hotel stands."

"I so love looking out at the water from my apartment window, early in the mornings."

Ritvik looked at her, imagining how she would appear early in the morning, her eyes sleepy and her face free of makeup. What kind of a night dress would she wear? He brought his wayward imagination under control with a conscious effort. As he removed his wallet to pay the bill, Sia opened her handbag, saying, "Let's split the expenses."

"No Sia. Allow me. It's my treat in return for that wonderful head massage which you gave me today. You see," he turned his head one way and then the other, "the pain has gone away completely."

Sia gave him a happy smile. "So glad to hear that. But then, I was only doing my job. Do let me share the bill." There was a mutinous set to her lips.

Not keen to get into an argument, Ritvik let her pay half of the bill which totalled to about eleven hundred rupees.

Ritvik took a longer route on their way back, showing Sia a little more of Udaipur, before he stopped the car at the entrance to Monarch. It was obvious that both were reluctant to part ways when Sia opened the car door. She got out and was surprised to find him standing next to her. A hand at her throat, she spoke in a choked whisper, "Thank you so much, Ritvik. I had a great time. Your car is simply adorable and I so enjoyed the ride in it."

"Hmm..." Ritvik looked down at her, a smile crinkling the corners of his eyes. "Thank you for going with me. Good night!" He drew an index finger down her left cheek in a fleeting stroke. Before Sia could respond or react, Ritvik turned around, got into his car, and drove away.

Sia stared after him, her hand to her cheek, her heart going into palpitations as she could still feel the heat of his touch. It had taken some time and a lot of effort to come to terms with spending time in Ritvik's company. But everything had gone to naught at that little touch. A deep sigh shuddered through Sia as she turned and walked into her building.

Later that night, Ritvik placed some cash in an envelope, along with a brief 'thank you' note, sealed it, wrote Sia's name on it, and left it at the hotel reception to have it delivered to her at Cleopatra's first thing in the morning.

Ritvik walked away, smiling to himself as he took the stairs two at a time on the way to his suite. If he knew Sia, there would be hell to pay tomorrow. And how he looked forward to the showdown!

Sia was surprised to receive a sealed envelope with her name written on it the moment she arrived at the salon. The handwriting was bold and masculine, she thought as she opened the cover carefully. Out tumbled two crisp two-thousand-rupee notes and a small business card with Ritvik Bansal's name on it. The smile disappeared from her face and her expression turned grim as Sia flipped the card to read what was written on the reverse.

"A small token for services rendered. Thanks, RB."

Her temper flaring out of control, Sia tore the card across and shoved it back into the cover along with the money. She wanted to rush over to wherever he was and throw the cover on Ritvik's face. The only problem was, she had three appointments lined up that morning. Her face tight and angry, unlike her usual self, Sia went about attending to her clients, seething from inside. The moment she was done with her last client of the morning, she removed her apron, brushed back her hair and walked out of the salon, not saying anything to her colleagues who watched her with surprise on their faces. It was indeed unusual behaviour for Sia to be so quiet and unfriendly.

"Hello, Sunil." Sia greeted the duty officer who was at the reception with a small smile. "Where will I find Mr Bansal?"

"Hello Sia. Ritvik must be in his office. Do you know where it is?"

She nodded, before asking, "Is someone with him?"

"I don't think so. Do you want me to call him to find out?"

"Don't bother, Sunil. I just want to see him for a few seconds. I'll just go and knock on his door. Thanks." She walked towards the far end of the reception and barged into the CEO's cabin. Relieved to confirm that he was indeed alone, Sia went in and shut the door firmly behind her.

"Hey Sia, good to see you! How have you been?" Ritvik greeted her with a wide grin.

Sia wanted to claw his handsome face as she glowered at him, not uttering a word, her eyes more silver than grey today morning.

"What happened? Is something wrong?" Ritvik spoke again. "Do take a seat. Let me order some coffee. Or would you prefer tea?" She looked delicious as the tempestuous heat added lustre to her face.

Sia went and stood in front of his table, showing him the cover. "What's the meaning of this?"

"Of what?" Ritvik pretended not to understand before his eyes shifted from her angry face to the envelope. He looked back at her again and said, "That! Well, I didn't tip you after that fabulous massage. I remembered later and hence left the money for you."

"How dare you?" Sia's voice turned hoarse, choking with hurt and anger.

Ritvik got up from his chair and walked over to her. "Why Sia? Isn't that the norm? Being the owner of this set up, I don't even have bills to pay. I should at least tip generously for the services, right?" His dark-as-devil eyes studied her minutely, watching every nuance in her expression.

"I was only doing my job for which I'm paid a damn good salary." She threw the cover on the table and turned around to walk out. The man she had had dinner with had been friendly and easygoing. The one who faced her today was the suave CEO of Maharaja International. How did she even imagine that she could be friends with him?

"Sia!"

She stopped in her tracks but didn't turn around as she didn't want him to see the tears shimmering in her eyes. She jerked away when he placed a hand on her shoulder.

"Listen." Ritvik's voice was soft while his breath teased her ear. He was standing too close for comfort, but she couldn't bring herself to move away. "I hope you wouldn't let your pride come in the way every time. Yesterday, I invited you out to dinner to get to know you more. It was also a means of saying 'thank you' for the massage. But you insisted on paying your way. I accepted your decision, didn't I?"

Sia turned around slowly, the hurt leaving her face and the pressure lifting from her heart as she stared up at Ritvik, light dawning in her gaze. "I..."

"I thought it only fair to leave you a tip since you wouldn't let me buy you dinner. Was I wrong?" He turned to his table, removing some tissues and handing them to her. "You're crying. Am I such an ogre?" he asked, tongue-in-cheek, his black gaze growing hotter by the second.

Sia shook her head, a glimmer of a smile shining from her eyes as she wiped her tears. "I feel so stupid. I don't know what to say!" Red tinged her cheeks as she felt embarrassed, what with her deep attraction towards him warring with her pride and temper—the whole gamut of emotions throwing her into a state of confusion. With the disappearance of her anger, Sia suddenly became extremely aware of their proximity. There was barely an inch of space between them and it looked like her body had become aware of it way before her mind.

It certainly was the case, for Sia could feel that her body had taken over her mind. She watched in morbid fascination as her arms lifted of their own accord and went around his neck, pulling his head down to hers while her lips pressed to his masculine ones, revelling in the touch. Sia forgot herself, let alone her surroundings, as she traced her tongue over the seam of his lips, seeking entry, sighing deeply when she got what she sought.

The smile disappeared from Ritvik's face as he clamped his arms around her waist, pulling her close to his hard body even as he let her tongue into his mouth. God! But she tasted delicious. They kissed as if there was no tomorrow, their tongues playing a duel, their hands running over each other. It was a while before they came up for air.

Sia opened her eyes slowly, as if coming out of a deep trance. Horrified at what she had done, she removed her hands in a hurry to press them against her mouth, her eyes wide as they stared at him. Ritvik's tie was askew while many of the buttons on his shirt were open and his hair had come undone from his man bun. "I..." Sia shook her head.

Ritvik laughed, his shoulders shaking with mirth. He still held her loosely in his arms, refusing to let her go when she tried her best to get out of his hold. "Women have thrown themselves at me a few times. But they were nothing like you, Sia. Your kiss sure packs a punch," he teased, winking at her. If anything, Sia's face turned redder, making him laugh some more.

"I..."

"That's the third time you've been stuck for words. I'm thrilled to note that I've managed to render you speechless." Ritvik grinned at her.

What has come over me? Sia had never, ever behaved like this. Not with anyone! *Have I gone mad?* How did she even think that she could kiss the man just because they had had dinner together last night? Yes, she desired him. Did that mean that she could just kiss him? She tried to get out of Ritvik's hold once again, only he wouldn't budge. "Please let me go." Her voice came out in a squeak.

"Don't plan to, now that I've got you exactly where I want you." Ritvik kissed her on her cheek. "Don't tell me you don't want to be in my arms anymore." He tried to pull her close to his chest, but she resisted.

"Ritvik." Sia turned her head the other way, her hands flat on his chest as she tried to push him away. Not having access to her mouth, he just continued to press soft and sensual kisses down the line of her neck, making her want to stop resisting and simply melt into his arms. But her mind had turned boss now, overpowering her body. She had to stop this. He was the owner of the 5-star hotel where she was only an employee. What must he think of her, the way she had initiated the kiss? Sia shut her eyes, shame-faced at her behaviour.

"Sia..." Ritvik lifted her chin to look down at her face. She opened her eyes a slit and he was amazed to see the fire burning in the depths of her smoky grey gaze. He was also delighted that she obviously wanted him as much as he needed her. "I'm going to kiss you again," he warned before leaning down to claim her lips in a searing kiss. Unable to resist, Sia gave up the fight and surrendered to the moment.

When they came up for air a second time, Sia moved a couple of feet away. She wasn't as awkward as she was before, but still... "I have no excuse for the way I behaved, Ritvik. I'll go now and won't embarrass you anymore."

"What?! Who said anything about my being embarrassed?" He slowly and deliberately pushed the buttons on his shirt into their holes, his eyes roving over her face and lissom body.

"Well, I did literally throw myself into your arms." Sia's voice was stronger now as she ran her hands over her hair, doing her best to bring some order to it. "I don't know what came over me. I've never done anything like this before."

"I'm glad to hear that." Ritvik's voice shook with laughter as he ran his hot gaze over her luscious lips. She looked so innocent and confused. If it had been midnight instead of midmorning, he would have finished what they had started. But he had a Skype call to take before meeting his little girl for lunch.

"Will you be serious, please?" Sia glared at him or at least tried to. But her eyes clung to his face, desire sparking in them once again.

"Okay. I'm serious now. Why did you kiss me?"

Sia looked at his unsmiling face and noticed the mischief lurking right at the back of his eyes. What the hell! She decided to be her honest self. "I'm terribly attracted to you, Ritvik. I..." Sia looked down at her feet.

"Is that so terrible?"

Confused, she frowned up at him. "What? I don't understand..."

"You said you're *terribly* attracted to me." His gorgeous lips stretched into a grin as he stressed the word.

Sia threw her arms up in the air. "I suppose I can't blame you for teasing me. I did behave like a slut." Her lips drooped.

"Totally!"

She looked up at him, her gaze shocked. Had he just agreed with her?

Unable to stop himself, Ritvik pulled her into his arms, pressing his lips to hers in a brief but explosive kiss. "You don't know how much of a turn on that is, you behaving like a slut, as you call it. I wouldn't dream of using the word though. I would say you're honest enough to own to your desires," he whispered in her ear. "Now get on with you." He patted her bottom. "Let's get together after work. Eight o'clock?" He raised an eyebrow at her.

She nodded, turning towards the door. It looked like she was going to like him a lot, even more than lusting after his sexy body.

"You might want to use the mirror in my washroom." Ritvik's laughter followed Sia all the way as she rushed into the washroom at the back of his cabin.

Sia couldn't stop grinning at her reflection in the mirror. Her curly hair was blowing in all directions while her lips were swollen from the kisses they had shared and her shirt had come out completely from her trousers. She quickly set right her clothes and face as much as she could before stepping back into

Ritvik's office. He was talking on the phone, all traces of mischief gone from his face. It was obviously an official call. Sia walked up to him swiftly and kissed him fully on his startled mouth before walking to the door. When she turned around to give him a wink and a wave, Ritvik's black gaze promised retribution.

Sia couldn't wait for the work day to be over.

khil Shetty raised a hand to acknowledge his boss when Ritvik passed through the reception on his way out, even as he handled the new batch of guests. A group of sixteen people had arrived from the USA, planning to spend a whole week in Udaipur. They had already booked their rooms online and were waiting for the formalities to be completed. The front office manager had set Dino, one of the duty officers, to complete the task while he organised their welcome drinks.

Akhil had come a long way from his days as a management trainee at Simha International in Mumbai. He used to be an angry young man those days, terribly jealous of Rohit Bansal, the managing director of Simha. It was all thanks to Ritvik that Akhil was where he was today, professionally and personally.

Akhil Shetty couldn't help recalling the scene that day when Rohit Bansal threw a party for his family...

It was only later when Akhil got to know what the celebration had been about. When he had been expecting the old director Baidyanath Thakkar and his daughter Muskaan to create a lot of trouble for Rohit, the latter had actually turned the tables on them and quietly bought their share of Simha International, thus removing them from the board. While it had been a matter of triumph to Rohit, it had only made Akhil burn with envy all the more. Over and above all that, the beautiful Tasha had also fallen in love with Rohit, making Akhil hate the man.

Akhil fumed as he watched Rohit's parents and siblings arriving for the party. Why did all great things happen only to the rich? Why not to middle-class people like Akhil who was born with a plastic spoon? Rohit Bansal was too handsome for his own good, a billionaire, ran a fabulous 5-star hotel in the heart of Mumbai, obviously had a secure family life and now he had a lovely woman for a partner.

Akhil, on the other hand, lived with his mother on the wrong side of the tracks. His father had left the two of them when Akhil had been barely two. His mother used to work as a housemaid to feed them both. It was a stroke of luck that Akhil had excelled at school, received a scholarship to complete a two-year stint at Hotel Management from a government recognised institute in Mumbai, and eventually landed a job as a management trainee at Simha International. He had felt such a powerful feeling of envy when he met Rohit Bansal for the first time. He couldn't help comparing the two of them all the time. Rohit's life had been a bed of roses, or that's what Akhil had presumed, while his own had been full of thorns. He had another month to go before his confirmation and promotion at the hotel.

"Hey, are you Akhil Shetty?" A tall man, standing in front of the reception desk, the morning after Rohit's party, asked him.

"Yes sir. How may I help you?" Akhil had responded politely, his face free of expression.

"Hey buddy, good to meet you. I'm Ritvik Bansal, Rohit's brother."

No wonder the man had seemed familiar. But the long hair and beard had stopped Akhil from making an instant connection. "Hello Mr Bansal, nice to meet you. I'm sorry I didn't recognise you." Akhil's smile didn't reach his eyes which had a permanently sad look in them.

"Call me Ritvik *yaar*. Are you terribly busy? Or can you go with me for a cup of coffee?"

Akhil had given him a surprised look. Rohit had always been formal with him. But his brother Ritvik was so friendly. "Sure, Ritvik. Can you give me five minutes? I just need to complete something and I can join you immediately after that."

"Perfect. I'll be waiting for you at The Pride. See you soon."

Not really knowing what to expect, Akhil had left in exactly five minutes to join Ritvik in the 24-hour coffee shop at Simha.

They had placed their order for their coffees before sitting back on the settee. "Listen, let me come straight to the point. You probably know that I run a 5-star hotel in Udaipur." Ritvik had looked at Akhil enquiringly.

"Yes, I do. Maharaja International, right?"

"Bingo." Ritvik grinned in appreciation. "I heard a lot about you from both my brother Rohit and Prisha Lohia from human resources. And I have a few questions to ask you too."

"I hope all good things, sir." Ritvik was being very nice to him. But never having been very confident, Akhil was worried what Rohit and Prisha must have said about him.

"Not just good, but great things. Listen, do call me Ritvik. I kinda get confused when someone calls me 'sir' okay?" Mischief glowed in Ritvik's eyes as he grinned again at Akhil. "I heard that you welcome responsibility and work all hours here at *Simha*."

Akhil sat up straight, his confidence going up a notch. His work had been noticed. While he had disliked Rohit from the bottom of his heart—it was his jealousy speaking of course—Akhil had always been an honest and hardworking employee. And he was also desperate to rise up the ladder as quickly as possible. Always having had to count his pennies, Akhil wanted to lead a luxurious life. He wanted to give his mother all those things which she had never had in her life. He nodded now. "Yes Ritvik. I like my job and I believe in hard work."

"Glad to know. Are you game shifting elsewhere or do you want to remain in Mumbai?"

"I don't understand." While Akhil's heart had gone mad with excitement, his cautious nature wouldn't let him presume too much.

"*Arre yaar*, I'm offering you a position in my hotel. It's still a baby, about a year old. New city, new way of handling things, though I think you'll be able to manage pretty well from the feedback I got from Prisha here. I..."

Akhil remembered keeping his coffee cup on the table carefully before taking both of Ritvik's hands in his. "Do you mean it?" A shimmer of tears surfaced in his eyes.

"Come on, buddy. You don't even know what the position is or what package I'm offering you. You should..."

"I'll take it." Akhil had always gone with his gut. Being cautious had become second nature because of his lack of confidence. But his instincts were strong. He had liked Ritvik the moment he met him. He felt friendly with Ritvik instead of the acrimonious jealousy he felt for his older brother.

Ritvik had laughed at Akhil's eagerness. "At least read your contract before signing it." He got up, shaking Akhil's hand. "I'll be seeing you in Udaipur in two weeks then. Welcome on board Maharaja International, Akhil Shetty. You are to be my front office manager."

Ritvik laughed when Akhil's mouth fell wide open in astonishment.

The trust Ritvik had placed in Akhil gave the latter a tremendous boost to his confidence. He spoke to Prisha at length before signing the contract for his new job. He didn't have to give his resignation since his term as management trainee was getting over anyway. Armed with a glowing letter of recommendation, Akhil waved goodbye to Mumbai and caught a flight to Udaipur along with his mother, their worldly belongings packed into two small suitcases. Yes, there wasn't all that much which belonged to them.

Akhil was touched when he arrived in Udaipur to be received by a car from Maharaja International which had whisked the two of them to a luxurious three-bedroom-hall-kitchen apartment on the top floor of Sovereign which was to be their home during his tenure at the hotel.

Only after receiving his first salary into his bank account could Akhil really believe that his luck had changed for the better, and how!

Ritvik had Akhil Shetty's gratitude, loyalty and friendship for life now, even as they ran the hotel splendidly between the two of them.

10

Ritvik got delayed at work and sent Sia a message, asking her to meet him at Kublai Khan, the oriental restaurant, on the first floor of Maharaja International, at 9.30 pm. Five of the restaurants were all accommodated one above the other while the sixth—the 24-hour coffee shop, Alexander the Great—occupied the whole of the terrace, around the skylight above the reception, with an amazing view of the Udai Sagar Lake from all four sides.

"Sorry about the delay, Sia. Something urgent came up." Ritvik greeted her with a hand at her elbow as he guided her to a secluded table for two near the window.

"Not at all," said Sia, sitting down on the luxurious and low-slung single sofa which was upholstered in silk with a pattern of dragons in red and gold, and just a dash of black. She felt torn between checking out the beautiful ambience even as her eyes kept flitting back to her host. "Oh, by the way, I don't think I can afford to share the bill here." She gave him a cheeky grin, hoping to ease the atmosphere which was fraught with sexual tension the moment she felt his touch at her elbow. It didn't really seem to matter where he touched her. How could a woman feel aroused when a man placed a hand at her elbow of all places?

Ritvik laughed. "Good." He handed a menu to her while giving his own a cursory glance before giving her his full attention. "Would you like to have some wine or maybe a cocktail?"

Sia grimaced. "I've never tasted alcohol. Let me avoid it for today since I need to be at work early tomorrow."

"Come on, Sia. Try a cocktail with not too much liquor. I'm sure you'll enjoy it. Coconut or strawberry? Which is your favourite?" His eyes danced in merriment as he looked at her. She was wearing a sleeveless, flowy dress in pale olive green which made her eyes appear lighter than usual. She was sitting back at ease on the sofa across from him. But he could see that it was all pretence as a pulse beat erratically at her throat while the colour ran high on her cheeks.

"Mmm... I like both actually. Do tell me what's on offer." Sia placed her elbows on the table and tucked her hands under her chin, running her sultry grey gaze over him.

"Pina Colada is made of coconut cream and pineapple juice with a dash of white rum. Strawberry Daiquiri also contains rum, lime juice and freshly crushed strawberries. We can order both. You taste and decide which one you prefer. What say?" A thick, dark eyebrow rose up in query.

Sia shook her head. "Not both. I'll have the pina colada. I'm sure it'll be yum."

Ritvik smiled. "Yeah, it's delicious." He turned to Karim who was waiting for their order. "Hello Karim. The lady will have a pina colada. Ask the bartender to go light on the rum. I'll have a Black Label whisky with lots of ice and soda."

"Sure, sir," smiled Karim, an admiring look in his eyes. He was in awe of his boss. "Some starters, sir?"

"Would you like some sushi?" Ritvik asked Sia.

"I'm an *anadi* when it comes to fine dining, Ritvik." Sia laughed unselfconsciously. "You order what you think is best. I've never tasted sushi before."

Ritvik forgot all about the hovering waiter as he watched her laugh, her head tossed back, giving him an untrammelled view of her long throat. She was growing on him, slowly and steadily. He turned to Karim and asked him to bring a sushi platter.

"Definitely, sir," said Karim, going away to place their order.

"So, when's your next day off?" Ritvik was keen to know.

"The day after tomorrow."

"Do you have plans?"

"I was thinking of doing a tour of the hotel. Right now, I have just seen the reception, the salon, the human resources office, and your cabin." Sia grinned at him.

"Would you like a guided tour by the owner?" Ritvik asked, his eyes roving over her face before settling on her wide lips, feeling a deep urge to have them under his.

"Do you think the owner will find time between his hectic schedule?" Sia fluttered her eyelashes at him, giving him a flirtatious glance.

Karim arrived with their drinks and placed them on the table. "The sushi should be ready in ten minutes, sir, ma'am."

Ritvik nodded, waving him off before raising his glass to Sia. "Cheers!"

"Cheers!" said Sia before taking a sip of her drink, her eyes going wide. "I've fallen in love with this pina colada," she declared, "It's truly delicious."

Ritvik watched her blissful expression, his own drink forgotten. Sia's face was a study in sensuality. The rest of the evening, he spent more time watching her eat, her face expressive as she savoured the food. She was a foodie through and through. It didn't matter that she had never had opportunities to eat at fine dine restaurants. Ritvik was excited about introducing her to different cuisines.

"You never did complete your story the other day." His velvety black gaze glowed with desire. "How did you manage to get to London and complete the beautician course there after your stints at those Delhi salons?"

Sia looked at Ritvik, her heart in her throat. He was wearing a black tuxedo teamed with a silver-grey bowtie and matching cummerbund. He had obviously changed for dinner. He was breathtakingly handsome, suave and courteous. He sure could turn a woman's head all around. She knew he was thirty-one. How was it that he was still single? She presumed he was since he had been flirting with her, though subtly, throughout the evening. "I was lucky that I came into some money which helped me fund the course. And as they say, the rest is history."

Ritvik noticed that her smile disappeared when she spoke about the money she had luckily come into. There was something there, but one look at her face and he curbed his curiosity for the time being. He planned to learn everything about her. But right now, he decided to put the smile back on her face. "Some history that, from the dingy beauty parlours of Delhi to a 5-star salon in Udaipur!" He raised his glass in a toast.

Colour rushed into Sia's cheeks as did the smile which had disappeared. "This bacon wrapped shrimp is superb."

"You should tell the head chef that. Huang Chang will be mighty pleased. We'll meet him when we're done here."

"Are you sure?" Sia suddenly felt shy. She had heard that chefs, especially the 5-star ones, had a lot of attitude.

"Of course! Why not?"

"He wouldn't mind? Chefs don't like to be disturbed, right?"

Ritvik laughed. "Not Chang. He loves to meet people."

And that's exactly what they did. Ritvik walked into the kitchen to hug the diminutive Chang. "Hey!

Sia's recently joined us as manager of Cleopatra's. She was keen to meet you. Sia," Ritvik held her hand to pull her forward, "Meet Huang Chang, the head chef of Kublai Khan."

"Hello Sia," said Chang, a smile on his chubby countenance, "Welcome on board."

"Thank you, Mr Huang. I must say that your culinary skills are amazing. I enjoyed every bite of what we had for dinner." Sia shook the head chef's hand enthusiastically.

Chang's smile turned to a grin. "Thank you, Sia. And you must call me Chang as we're colleagues."

Sia nodded at Chang happily. She felt pleasantly drunk after two rounds of the delicious cocktail.

"We won't keep you, Chang, as I can see that the restaurant's full. I'll be seeing you around," said Ritvik, waving to the chef as they turned around to leave.

Sia missed a step and was glad Ritvik was holding her hand. She giggled. "I think I'm drunk."

Ritvik let go off her hand to place an arm around her slender waist. "Drunk?" he asked, his voice amused as he stopped to look down at her, her head barely reaching his shoulder. "How could you get drunk on that itsy bit of rum?"

Sia giggled again. "I don't know. Just that my head is buzzing and I feel as if I'm floating above the ground." She leaned her head against his shoulder, trying her best to get her wits together. It must be the combination of one sexy male and that itsy bit of rum—it had gone to her head totally.

"You're probably tired after a long day." Ritvik felt bad that he had delayed dinner. It was 11.30 pm and she must be beat. She did spend a lot of time on her feet at the salon. He held her close to his side as they went down the staircase. "Let me take you home."

"I'd like that." Sia gave him a wide smile.

They walked the whole length of the drive, out through the imposing gates, and turned left towards the staff quarter which was barely a five-minute walk for Ritvik on normal days. But today, escorting a tipsy Sia took him a little more than that. Not that he minded as he matched his pace to her smaller steps.

When they reached an area which was dark, a large neem tree blocking the light from the streetlamps, Ritvik stopped to pull Sia into his arms. He placed a hand at her throat and wasn't too surprised to feel the pulse beating rapidly there. Lifting her face up to his, he pressed his mouth to the corner of her lips. "Sia..."

"Ritvik." Sia locked her arms around his neck to pull his head down to her, a deep sigh emanating from the depths of her being as he brushed his tongue over her lips. She opened her mouth to let him in, only to forget her own name.

It was a while before Ritvik lifted his head to look down at her. "I don't know about your being intoxicated, but I'm drunk on you," he whispered when she opened her eyes a slit to look at him. With a shuddering sigh, Ritvik controlled his libido and removed his arms from around her. When Sia protested, he laughed softly. "It's time you went home, honey. You have a full day tomorrow."

Sia made a face at him before taking a bite of his lower lip. Her tongue darted out to caress the spot when he winced. "I'm not going to apologise for that." Her silver-grey eyes challenged his charcoal gaze.

Ritvik laughed again. "I promise to get back at you when you're more awake." He took her hand as they turned to walk towards Monarch. He walked up with her to the second floor and waited for her to enter her apartment before wishing her 'good night'.

"Ritvik." Sia called to him as he walked away.

"What?" Ritvik turned his head to look at her. Sia was sinfully tempting as she leaned against the doorway.

"Nothing." Sia shook her head. "Good night." Colour ran up her cheeks at the expression in his eyes which seemed to devour her, as they ran from the top of her head to the tips of her toes peeping from her open-toed heels.

Ritvik blew her a kiss before taking the stairs two at a time, whistling softly under his breath.

11

Ritvik was too busy the next day and knew he wouldn't have time to meet Sia. But he had deliberately decided to complete a lot of work so that he could be free for a few hours the day after to take Sia on her promised tour of Maharaja International.

He started the day taking Aarya for a ride on Pinocchio, had breakfast with her and got ready for work. "Meera Aunty, please handle Aarya's lunch. What do you want to have, sweetie?" He turned to ask his daughter as he held her in his arms.

"Noodhles?" Aarya tilted her head to look at her father with a naughty smile.

"Not today, you imp. You had noodles only yesterday. How about *roti* and *sabzi* maybe? Meera Aunty can make you your favourite *mattar paneer*. Okay?"

Aarya nodded her head vigorously, her curls falling all over her face, making her giggle. "And two *rothi*. Okay?" She raised her index and middle finger to show her father. "Daddhie also eat?"

Ritvik shook his head, ruffling her hair. "Sorry sweetie. Daddy has to go out for a meeting today. We'll have dinner together. Meera Aunty will eat lunch with you."

"Okay." Aarya hugged her father close, giving him a noisy kiss. She wriggled from his arms to slide down to the floor. "Bye Daddhie. I'm goin' to play."

"Bye sweetie." Ritvik left even as Aarya trotted over to where her toys were.

Finding himself free for a few minutes at around 4 pm, he went to Cleopatra's. Sia was busy with a haircut when he entered, though she gave him a smile of welcome, making his heart go all mushy. He returned her smile before sitting down on a couch as he greeted Asha who was the only one free, sitting at the counter, a glossy magazine open on her lap.

"Hello Ritvik." Asha gave her boss a cheerful smile. She noted that he had been visiting the salon more often nowadays and was very well aware of the reason. The attraction between Ritvik and Sia stood out from a mile. "Come to meet Sia?" she asked cheekily.

Ritvik grinned. "Yes. Does she have an appointment lined up?"

Asha shook her head. "Nope, she's free for fifteen minutes before her next."

"Phew!" Ritvik looked at his watch. He planned to check on Aarya before his meeting with Senthil, the head chef of Rajaraja Chola at 4.30 pm.

"Would you like some coffee?"

"That'd be awesome. Thanks Asha." He got up. "I'll wait in Sia's cabin." The salon manager had a cabin to herself though she didn't use it much. But he wanted to meet Sia in private.

Asha called room service to place an order for coffee even as Sia finished with her client. "Ritvik's waiting for you in your office. You go on. I'll deal with the bill."

"Thanks Asha." Colour ran up Sia's cheeks as she walked into her cabin, calling out to Ritvik, "Hey, I thought you had a hectic schedule today."

Ritvik turned towards her from where he was standing at the window and pulled her into his arms. "I still do. But I needed a few minutes with you," he growled before pressing his lips against hers.

Sia threw her arms around his neck to pull him closer, opening her mouth for his kiss. Was she glad that he had made time for her! They pulled apart when there was a knock on the door. A waiter came in to place the coffee on the table and left immediately.

"Will you have some coffee too?" asked Ritvik, looking at Sia's red face.

"Hmm, okay."

He handed her a cup before sipping from his, his dark gaze roving over her. "You look sexy."

"So do you," said Sia, her grey eyes checking him out.

Colour ran up Ritvik's rugged cheeks as he said, "I'm glad I could meet you today." He placed his empty cup on the table, saying, "I'll take myself off." Just then, they heard something that sounded like a woman's scream. "What the fuck! Is that Fern do you think? Where's she?" asked Ritvik, rushing out of her door.

"She's giving a client a massage in cabin 5." Sia ran right behind him.

Ritvik opened the door of cabin 5 gently, just in case nothing was amiss. He saw red when he noticed the male client flashing his member at Fern even as he was pulling her hand to place it over him. "Fern!"

"Ritvik!" Fern was sobbing as she rushed into his arms. "I... I..."

Ritvik patted her on her back before pushing her gently into Sia's arms. "Take her away, Sia. Let me deal with this scum." Ritvik didn't wait to see if the women had left before walking to the massage table and giving the man a hard slap.

The man got up, his face red with anger as he held a hand over his cheek. "How dare you? You don't know who I am. I'll..."

"I don't care. Just get out of here," Ritvik snarled.

The man cowered, staring at the snarling giant warily. Pulling on his clothes in a hurry, he said, "You don't know the clout I wield. You'll be sorry for this."

"Go do your best."

"I'm booked in this hotel for a whole week. I'll complain to your boss. I..."

"What's your name, you jerk?" He turned around to see Akhil standing at the door. "There you are. Akhil..."

"Mr Shetty, you've got to tell this man who I am. His behaviour's atrocious. I want to meet the owner of this hotel and place a complaint against the man."

"Mr Janardhan is in import export," Akhil spoke to Ritvik, a twinkle in his eye. "He arrived today and is booked to stay for the whole week."

"Check him out this minute and return his advance. He's not going back to his room. Send someone to pack his bags. I'll let you deal with it, Akhil. I'm getting late for my meeting."

"Sure, no worries."

"Who the hell is he? I'm going nowhere. I paid an advance..." Janardhan was shouting at the top of his voice when Akhil firmly escorted him out of the salon.

Ritvik went back into Sia's cabin when he found out that's where she had taken Fern, who was sitting, sipping from a mug of hot tea. He went and knelt down on the floor next to Fern. "I'm really sorry about that, Fern. I don't know what to say." He held her hand, looking up at her.

Fern's eyes shimmered with tears. She sniffed, smiling through her tears. "It's okay now. I'm so glad you were around."

"Do you want to take the day off? I think I'll hire a bouncer for taking care of you girls. What do you think, Sia?" He turned to ask her.

Sia appeared to come out of a trance. Her attraction for Ritvik had turned into full fledged love the moment she saw the concern he was showing for young Fern. How could she not fall in love with the man?! He was totally adorable.

"I think it would be for the best." Sia sighed. The incident had shaken her up and she wasn't even directly involved. She felt terrible for Fern.

"Tell you what! Unless you girls have back-to-back appointments, why don't you three take off for a film or something? And dinner maybe. Take a hotel car and send the bill to Akhil. Let Andy and Inder deal with what work is left over for the day. See if you need to cancel some appointments. Go on. I'm sure you can do with a change of scene."

"It's okay, Ritvik..."

He didn't allow Fern to complete the sentence. "It's not okay. I've let that bastard get off too easily. Sia, you heard me. Take the rest of the day off. Let the men run the salon for the rest of the day."

Sia nodded, her eyes glowing with love for him. "Thank you, Ritvik. I think you're right. We'll take off for the day."

"Good girl." He patted her cheek. "You take care, Fern." Ritvik ruffled her hair as he would have done Aarya's. Looking at his watch, he said, "Shit. I'm late. See you all."

Sia watched him go, her heart in her eyes.

Ritvik quickly dialled Senthil. It was 4.45 and the head chef had a temper. "Hello Senthil. I'm sorry I got a bit delayed with an emergency. I'm walking to your kitchen as we talk." Rajaraja Chola, the restaurant on the fourth floor serving South Indian cuisine, was Senthil's territory. The forty-two-year-old had come highly recommended by Ritvik's sister Rhea. Senthil used to work as junior chef in Rose Garden International's Chettinad restaurant called Bugatti. The man had both, a temper and loads of attitude. Ritvik put up with his tantrums only because he was not just a fabulous chef, but also very good at managing the restaurant. The customers came again and again and the three thousand square feet restaurant was always full. Senthil thrived on work and rarely took a day off. The HR had to press him to take a couple of weeks off every year.

"Ritvik, I did wonder and almost called you. But then, I know how busy you are and decided to wait for exactly fifteen minutes before beginning preparations for dinner."

"So glad I caught you before you did that, Senthil. See you." Ritvik entered the kitchen even as he cut the call. The two men shook hands before they sat down with a cup of coffee at one of the restaurant tables. No hugs for Senthil; he had frowned heavily when Ritvik had hugged him the only time he had.

"So, tell me your requirements," said Ritvik, getting to the point immediately.

The meeting was over in twenty minutes, giving Ritvik enough time to go meet Aarya.

"Thanks, Ritvik." Senthil gave him a rare smile. "I like the way you take decisions so quickly."

Armed with a compliment that was as scarce as Senthil's smile, Ritvik took the stairs to the third floor with a grin on his face, as he wondered what Sia would have to say about Senthil's attitude.

12

Akhil instructed Dino to supervise the packing of Janardhan's luggage as he got the bill readied. "I wish Ritvik would let me levy a fine for what the bastard did." Akhil muttered to Sunil as he clicked the page on the computer. "Sunil, you take care of this. I'd better go and take control of the situation." Akhil left the reception desk as Sunil nodded, keenly watching Janardhan as he stepped out of the washroom on the left side.

Though Janardhan had done his best to do repairs, the left side of his face was puffed up and red. He was beyond angry. Who the hell was that guy? How had he dared to touch him? Janardhan conveniently forgot all about the inappropriate touching he had tried to force the masseuse into. He planned to drag the hotel's name through mud. He had connections in the media. He walked forward, only to find the front office manager blocking his path. "Please wait a few minutes, Mr Janardhan. We'll have your luggage brought down and also reimburse the balance of your advance to your credit card."

Janardhan glared at the front office manager. "What balance? I want my whole money back."

Akhil gave the man a polite smile, gritting his teeth. "That won't be possible, mister." No way was he going to address the man as 'sir'. "You have already used the room and items from the mini bar. Then there's the massage and..."

"What massage?" Janardhan shouted, making heads turn in their direction. Though the area was really large, it was crowded enough as the hotel was running full, with also guests who had turned up to have meals at the many restaurants. "The bitch didn't give me a massage."

"Through no fault of hers." Akhil's voice was firm.

"I need to speak to your boss. I want to complain about that man who dared to enter the private cabin at the salon. How could he...?" Janardhan was still shouting.

"The CEO's in a meeting. It won't be possible for you to meet him." Akhil would have been overjoyed to tell the bastard that it was his boss who had slapped him. He refrained himself with difficulty. He knew for a fact that Ritvik wouldn't want it broadcasted that the CEO of the hotel was capable of slapping a guest. If quoted out of context, it could spoil the hotel's reputation.

Janardhan turned his tactics. "Tell me something, Akhil. That girl who gave me a massage, she's Fern, right?" Akhil gave an imperceptible nod, gritting his teeth, before the man continued conversationally, "Don't you think she's kind of innocent for the job?

I don't think she's had much experience with men. She…"

Akhil locked his hands behind his back as they itched to have a go at the other man. What a bastard! "Tell me something, Mr Janardhan," he spoke mildly, "Is this your first stay at a 5-star hotel?"

"What do you mean by that?" Janardhan's face had gone a strange shade of puce as he glared at Akhil.

"It's just that we run a world-class, reputed hotel here, mister, not a brothel. How dare you?" Akhil turned to the reception and spoke to Sunil, "Are we ready with the bills, Sunil?"

"Yes sir. I've credited the balance to Mr Janardhan's credit card."

Just then, Som from housekeeping walked out of the elevator with a suitcase and a carry bag. He placed the luggage in the bellhop's trolley and reported to Sunil that the luggage from room 326—Janardhan's— had been brought down.

"Here you go." Akhil handed over the envelope with his bills over to Janardhan. "Your luggage is down. Please go and don't ever show your face here again."

"I have a good mind to go to consumer court."

"You must do what you think is right, mister." Akhil turned away, without bothering to wish him a good day. He called security and instructed them to make sure that Janardhan left the premises.

Realising that he wasn't going to get help from anyone, Janardhan turned to leave when he saw Ritvik step down the staircase into the reception. He rushed over to him and caught him by his collar. "Come right now. I don't care if the CEO is in a meeting; I need to complain about you. How dare you take matters into your hands? It's no business of yours, stepping into the salon and beating me up. I..."

"Take your hands off me unless you're eager to be slapped again. Maybe on the other cheek this time?" Ritvik looked at the man as if he was eyeing the dirt under his shoes.

Meghnath, one of the bouncers, appeared next to them the very next instant, towering over even Ritvik's six feet, three inches height. "Do you need help, boss?"

Janardhan reluctantly let go of Ritvik's collar, turning left and then right as he eyed both men. He felt puny beside them. "Boss?" He asked the bouncer with a heavy frown. Turning to Ritvik, he said, "I wonder what makes you think you have the run of the place? Your hired man is also running amok here." He turned and shouted to Akhil, "Hey Shetty, show me the way to your CEO. I need to report this."

Meghnath bodily lifted Janardhan, walked swiftly to the entrance and dumped him outside the building. "You are an idiot. It's the CEO you were trying to manhandle. Get out and stay out, do you hear?" His voice was soft for such a huge man, but the look in his fiery eyes was enough to shut Janardhan up finally.

Shoulders drooped in defeat, Janardhan walked away, dragging his suitcase behind him.

Pretty cheerful and upbeat by nature, Fern came out of her blues pretty fast, especially after Sia and Asha thought up different methods to bring harm to Janardhan's genitals. The three of them cackled all the way to Celebration Mall to check out the movies running there. Sia booked tickets for *Ek Haseena Thi Ek Deewana Tha* at PVR. With minutes to spare, they picked up tubs of popcorn and iced teas before finding their seats.

The film was just okay and the girls continued to crack jokes, confident of not disturbing the rest of the audience as there were but a few people, sitting far apart from them. The outing had done not just Fern, but all three of them a lot of good. That's when Sia decided that they should do this at least once a month, to keep their morale up.

They had an awesome meal at Barbeque Nation on the third floor of the mall, their girlie chat continuing over cocktails and the barbequed bites which were grilled right there at their table. It was way past ten when they got up to leave after helping themselves to the sumptuous buffet. They dropped Asha outside her home before going on to the staff quarters.

"Do you think you'll be alright by yourself? Or you can sleep over at my apartment tonight," offered Sia, a hand on Fern's shoulder when they stopped outside Magnate, the building where the latter lived.

Fern smiled, patting Sia's hand. "I'm truly fine now. At that moment, it was a shock. But I don't plan to cry over that jerk's psychotic behaviour."

"Proud of you, Fern." Sia gave her a hug before walking up the stairs to her apartment, a smile on her face. She messaged Ritvik, telling him that Fern was fine.

Sia couldn't wait to meet him the next day, her day off. She had offered to swap with Fern, but the other girl had refused. "I just had an off two days back. I like my job and would rather work then do something else."

Ritvik called Sia immediately. "Hey."

"Hi, I just sent you a message." Sia's voice was choked when her heart jumped into her throat on hearing his voice.

"I am calling you after seeing it. Did you girls have fun?"

"You don't know how much," laughed Sia.

"Don't make me jealous now."

Sia hooted with laughter as she fell on her bed, rolling from side to side as she held the phone against her ear.

"What's so funny?" Ritvik grumbled, even as his smile became wider. Her laughter was infectious.

"The thought of you being jealous of the three of us." Sia sobered enough to say, "I've been thinking. What about some self-defence classes for the girls?"

"Hmm... not a bad idea. Let me think about it."

"Yes please. Though I think you should agree. I'm a karate blue belt. Believe me, it's useful." With difficulty, she controlled her voice which threatened to wobble.

"Sia? Wanna tell me more?" Ritvik sensed that she was disturbed. The woman was full of surprises.

"Maybe some other time. Listen," Keen to change the subject, Sia asked, "Are you going to give me the grand tour tomorrow? I did ask Fern if she wanted to have the day off instead of me, but she refused."

"Aww, you didn't have to do that, Sia. You deserve a break too. And yes, I am. Let's meet at ten. Come over to my office."

"Will do that."

"Did you miss me at all when you went gallivanting around town today?"

"Hmm... let me think." Sia paused, a wide grin on her face as she wondered at his expression. He sounded bugged. "Truth?"

"As if I would want anything else," Ritvik growled.

"I miss you every second that I'm not with you," Sia whispered into the phone, "I miss your arms around me. I miss your lips on mine. I..."

"Sh... sh... no more. I'll come over." He had gone painfully hard just listening to her.

Sia laughed softly. "No, no, please don't. Let me have my beauty sleep. I need to look fresh for my tour with the boss tomorrow." She was pretty tired after the hectic morning, followed by the drama and then the outing. And more than that, what was happening between Ritvik and her was still too new.

"Ouch!" The lady was definitely in command. "You do realise it isn't going to be so easy to put me off tomorrow, don't you?"

"Who wants to put you off? Didn't I just tell you how much I miss you..."

"Nope. I don't want to hear about it, not again. I don't think my body can take more of it." Ritvik groaned. "I'll let you show me tomorrow."

"It's a date. Goodnight." Sia disconnected the phone, laughing softly to herself. She loved him!

Ritvik stared at his phone, his scowl turning into a smile. He looked forward to tomorrow. He had never met anyone like her, ever. Sia was unique!

13

itvik waved Sia into a chair when she walked into his office the next morning sharp at ten, as he was speaking on the phone. Her eyes took on a mischievous glint as she mouthed, "Coffee?"

When Ritvik nodded, she called room service and placed the order, sitting back demurely in her chair, studying Ritvik.

He was casually dressed today, the top two buttons of his white linen shirt left open, giving her a glimpse of the hair on his chest. She pressed two fingers to her lips and blew him a kiss and was surprised to see the ruddy colour rushing up his face, even as Ritvik swung his chair to look away from her. Sia smiled to herself, not too bothered that he had turned away. She knew that she was distracting him. The call was obviously important or he wouldn't still be on the phone. She studied the right side of his face. His nose was regally patrician, which only added to his looks. His ear was red now, tempting her to take a bite.

Ritvik caught the desire in her gaze when he turned suddenly after disconnecting his call. A dark eyebrow went up as he studied her with his burning charcoal gaze. Sia was wearing jeans and a sleeveless top of yellow and green. Her face was glowing with no makeup. His eyes lingered over her shapely breasts for a whole minute, making her go red. A wide grin split his face at her reaction. Deepak walked in just then and placed the coffee tray on the desk. Ritvik nodded his thanks and waited for the man to leave before getting up from his chair.

He pulled Sia from her chair and into his arms, taking her hand and placing it against his crotch. "Have you any idea how uncomfortable it can be if my shaft remains that way for hours on end?" He growled, stroking his tongue against the hard beating pulse at her throat.

Sia ran a caressing hand over him, turning her head to give him better access as he nibbled her neck. "You poor baby!" Her voice was shaking with laughter as Sia spoke into the ear which she had been admiring from afar before she took a sharp nip of his lobe. She rubbed the spot with her tongue even as she felt him grow harder against her caressing palm.

Ritvik's hands pressed against her luscious bottom as he pulled her closer against his aroused body. "I need you, honey."

Sia moved away to look up at him, her dark pupils gone wide with desire. She traced her forefinger over his shirt collar, moving it out of the way before pressing her lips to his hair roughened chest.

Silence reigned there for a few minutes before Ritvik lifted his head to look at Sia. "You won't get to see the hotel at this rate." With a shaky grin, he pushed her back into the chair before buttoning his shirt. Ritvik was surprised to find that his hands were quite steady as he poured the coffee into two cups. "Here you go." He handed her a cup before drinking from his own as he sat on the corner of his table close to her.

Ritvik got up the moment Sia finished her coffee. Placing a hand under her elbow, he said, "Let's go."

They walked to where the reception desk was, manned by Dino. "This whole area was an open courtyard. You see the fountain in the centre? It has been there since the time the palace was completed in 1580. I had the original patched up and running once again. Obviously, we needed to cover the area and hence the skylight."

Sia looked way up at the skylight which was five floors above. The natural light created the perfect ambience for the heritage hotel's front hall. She turned to look at the life size portrait of a man and woman beside the reception desk. "Are they the once-upon-a-time rulers of this place?"

Ritvik grinned, shaking his head. "They are my parents, Alok and Menaka Bansal." At Sia's look of astonishment, he continued, "Well, the hotel used to be a palace and I have retained the history as much as possible. But at the end of the day, it's my space. I didn't want pictures of the Thakore family. That's when the idea struck me. I had my parents wear royal clothes and their photos taken professionally. It wasn't difficult for an artist to paint this portrait after that."

"Brilliant!" Sia was impressed. "And I can relate to your sentiments."

"You'll also see some more pictures of the members of my family around." Ritvik winked.

"Yours too?"

Ritvik tilted his head in acknowledgement.

"This I must see." An imp of mischief danced in Sia's gaze.

Moving his gaze away from her face with an effort, Ritvik drew Sia's attention to the wall sconces which were designed to look like antiques but were from the local market. The palace had not been in the best of condition when he had purchased it. Rewiring had to been done after pulling down dreary and grotesque looking lamps.

"You know that Jhansi ki Rani is on the right."

"Yeah, I see it every day on my way to Cleopatra's."

"Ever been inside?" When Sia shook her head, he walked with her to the wide double doors of glass and carved wood and went in. It was too early for customers though they could hear the sounds of utensils and cutlery as the waiters got the tables ready. There were square tables for four all through the restaurant, the chairs with carved backs and fitted cushions. The colours were bright with shades of fiery orange and fuchsia pink over dull gold brocade. "They serve North Indian fare, leaning towards Rajasthani and Lucknowi specialities."

Sia nodded, absorbing it all. The grandeur was mind boggling to the woman from a small town.

They went to the bar and disco on the opposite side of Jhansi ki Rani, also on the ground floor. Basically, the four corners of the reception housed the restaurant, the disco, Cleopatra's and Ritvik's office.

The flooring in Prince Regent was of highly polished wood with bar stools along the perimeter. On one corner was the bar and on the other end was a stage for DJs and live musicians. There was an array of musical instruments arranged there, including a drum set and a keyboard. There were only the two cleaners working there, getting the disco ready for the day. "The bar opens at noon and the disco by around seven and is on till five in the morning."

They went to all the restaurants, one on each floor, bypassing Kublai Khan on the first as Sia had already been there. There was Emperor Akbar on the second floor renowned for its authentic Mughlai cuisine, just as its name suggested. Sia drew in a deep breath, loving the aroma wafting from the kitchen. Looking at her, Ritvik declared, "We'll have lunch here once we're done with the tour."

Sia nodded. "I'd love that."

He appreciated that there was no pretence or coyness in Sia. When she wanted something, she was pretty open about it.

As they went up the stairs to the third floor, Ritvik said, "The staircases were another thing we had to work on. They used to be narrow and steep. I think most palaces were built that way to keep enemies out or at least slow them down, if you know what I mean. I had them made wider and easier on the legs."

The brass board at the entrance read Louis IV in black. "French cuisine. You must try the lobster here some time and also the breads. Simply melt in the mouth!"

Sia nodded as she took in the elegant seating for twos, fours and sixes. A small bouquet of pink carnations was placed in a glass vase in the middle of every table flanked by tulip candle holders in glass and silver on both sides. The decor was stylish with the colour scheme of pastel green and blue. "Love the place. It looks so cool."

Ritvik gave her a quick kiss on her soft cheek, saying, "I'm glad to know."

He opened a suite—Queen of Hearts, it was called—with his master key to show her around. "Queen of Hearts. How cute! Whose idea was the theme?"

"Mine, helped along by my sis Rhea."

"Amazing."

Rajaraja Chola on the fourth floor made Sia's jaw drop. Having never been south of Delhi, she was astounded by the decor in the South Indian restaurant which was so different from what she had seen so far. Brass played a predominant role; a huge pot of the alloy was placed in the centre of the restaurant, and was filled to the brim with water with lilies of myriad colours floating in it. The wall sconces and two chandeliers were also made of brass and glass. There was a bell near the entrance which Ritvik raised a hand to ring. "Just something different to let the manager know when a new customer walks into the restaurant." No table lamps here. The whole place was brightly lit and the colour scheme was cream and gold.

"Now the chef here, Senthil, is the one with the attitude. He's excellent and has the typical temper which is associated with chefs," said Ritvik in a whisper. "He has a heart of gold but a sharp tongue."

Sia nodded. "Must be the kind who gives the other chefs like Huang Chang a bad name." Sia also spoke in a whisper, a shiver going up her spine. "So, what would you recommend here?" she asked.

"Every single item on the menu and I'm not being prejudiced here. You must try the full meal. It's something like our *thali*, but served on a banana leaf. There are twenty-four items served along with rice, *pappadam* and pickle."

Sia's eyes opened wide. "Twenty-four? Is that just for the one meal?"

Ritvik grinned. "Yes. The portions are small and you get to taste so many items from Tamil Nadu."

Sia went to a bronze plaque on the wall to read the history of the South Indian king Rajaraja Chola which was embossed in black on it. That was one of the fascinating things about the restaurants. Each one had the king or queen's history—the one it was named after—on display. Oh yes, there was one of Queen Cleopatra and her beauty secrets at her salon too.

On the fifth floor, Sia read out aloud. "Augustus Caesar, continental cuisine."

"Yes. The kitchen here also accommodates Alexander the Great on the terrace. That's the 24-hour coffee shop."

"Must be some job managing this huge operation." Sia looked at Ritvik, admiration evident in her grey gaze.

"It is, though I must say I thoroughly enjoy doing what I am doing. And then, my staff is the best. Akhil Shetty is an excellent second-in-command." Ritvik insisted on giving credit to them.

Though Sia nodded at what he said, she didn't completely agree. Ritvik was the dynamo which fired the set up. She could feel his passion as he showed off his hotel to her.

They finally reached the terrace. It was mostly open air with shades set up in certain sections. There were extra large terracotta pots with plants and small trees, making the place appear like a garden. "Guests like to sit here under the stars in the evening." He guided her towards the centre. "Have a look."

Sia stared at the huge sheet of glass fitted on the floor right in the middle of the terrace. Looking down, her jaw dropped when she noticed the centre fountain. It was the hotel's reception she was gazing at from up here. She ran around the periphery of the glass which was the same size as the reception, not really caring that the guests might look at her strangely. She could see people walking around the reception, looking like miniatures on the move. Truly fascinating!

When she raised her head to look at Ritvik admiringly, he laughed, saying, "You're yet to catch the view on the outside."

Sia shook her head. "I don't think you can offer anything better than this." But she realised how wrong she was when she went to the compound wall of the terrace and saw the green waters of the Udai Sagar Lake.

Ritvik pointed out other famous hotels which surrounded the lake. Their reflections shimmered in the clear waters. "You should come here in the evening to see the lights, a sight to behold."

Sia gave a deep and satisfied sigh. "That was the most amazing tour, Ritvik. I'm so glad that you could show me the place yourself."

"We aren't done yet." Ritvik grinned.

"There's more to see? Where?" Sia squealed. They were on the top floor and hence must have finished the tour is what she had thought.

"Come along." They took the elevator to the ground floor and went to his office cabin. Walking behind his desk, Ritvik pressed a finger to a small square button on the stone wall and a section of the wall slid open, making Sia's eyes go round.

"Is that a secret passage?" she asked in awe.

Ritvik gave her a grin as he stepped through the doorway, holding her hand. But there was enough space for only one person at a time. They found themselves at the top of a staircase which went down. He pressed something on the wall and the door to his office slid shut. Light came from a single window near them, showing them the way down. But there was only darkness further below.

"But Ritvik, your cabin is on the ground floor. Are you taking me to the dungeon?" Instead of horror, there was only excitement in Sia's voice.

Ritvik shrugged. "Not since the past century at least, though you're right. It was originally built as a dungeon. I'm going down first. Just follow me."

Sia's heart went pitter-patter as she walked down the narrow and curved staircase built of stone, with no railing. The steps were steep and there were twenty-two of them. Yes, she counted. Ritvik stepped down and pressed a switch and the chamber—that's what she wanted to call it—came to light along with the hum of an air-conditioner.

"Whoa!"

The ceiling was about ten feet, low by the standards of the rest of the hotel, though the room was big, at least five hundred feet square. It was decorated like a sitting room from the pages of history, with divans and antique sofas interspersed by low, carved tables. The walls were of rough stone and the light came from sconces of burnished copper. Sia walked closer to check them out and realised they were shaped like crowns.

"Is this the only room?" asked Sia, her voice a reverent whisper.

"There are two more. I've had them converted into bedrooms. Don't you think it makes for an intriguing holiday destination?" he grinned.

"Absolutely. So, is this also open for guests?" Sia sank into a squishy sofa, trying to absorb her surroundings. The finale was grander than everything else. It was truly breathtaking.

"Nope," he shook his head. "It's only for family and friends. Come along, let me show you the other rooms. You know, there used to be an underground tunnel which went all the way for two miles, most of it under the lake, to reach a similar chamber in the other palace where the Thakores live even today."

"What? You mean a real tunnel? I've only heard of those. This sounds like out of a movie. Is it still open?"

Ritvik laughed, shaking his head. "I had it shut up, the first thing I did when the renovation began."

Sia stopped mid-step, turning to look at him. "You sabotaged history," she declared, pretending to smite her forehead. "And Dayanita Thakore is really of royal lineage. I thought she was just bluffing her way through. Maybe I shouldn't have..."

Ritvik laughed. "No harm. The young lady keeps floating somewhere so high up in the clouds that it would do her a lot of good to be brought down to earth time and again." He winked at Sia as they entered the bedroom on the right.

There was a huge four-poster bed made of teakwood, carved beautifully. There was no doubt it was an antique. "It's from the 1700s," said Ritvik as if he could read her mind.

Sia had gone silent as she walked around the room. Oh yes, there was a lot of space around the cot, a wardrobe covering one wall, a wide dressing table made of brilliant white marble with gold veins, the mirror fitted into a wooden frame with carvings which exactly matched the bed and wardrobe. There were two single sofas with a round shaped carved table in between. Sia walked around, laying a hand on the sofa and then the bed, feeling the soft silk upholstery and sheets. They seemed to be from some other realm. She stopped before the painting of a man dressed in full fledged regalia, along with a sword encased in an intricately worked silver scabbard, suspended from his belt. It took her a few seconds to realise that it was Ritvik, his gorgeous man bun tucked into a golden turban. She drank in the sight, her throat choking. He was beautiful! No other word for it.

"Ritvik!" He walked closer to her, standing next to her as she studied the portrait from top to toe. "I want a picture of this. Do you mind?"

He shook his head, the smile disappearing from his face as he noticed the desire in hers. "Would you like me to click it for you?"

"Will you please?" Sia stood next to the portrait. "Do get me also in the frame."

Ritvik quickly clicked half a dozen shots from his iPhone, sending them to her by WhatsApp.

"Your hotel looks gorgeous."

"No more than you." Ritvik pulled her into his arms, nuzzling her cheek, dragging a damp tongue over her jaw line. "Sia... I want to make love to you, only if you're willing. I..."

Sia pressed her fingers against his masculine lips. "Yes, please."

Ritvik lifted her high up in his arms, his face buried against her breasts as he carried her to the bed and placed her in the centre of it. He straightened up to unbutton his shirt, only to have Sia push his hands away and take over.

Her grey gaze looked into his black eyes invitingly while her hands were busy with the task of pushing the shirt off his muscular shoulders.

Sia sat back on her haunches to simply stare at his stupendous form, her mouth wide open in an O. "Ritvik," she said in awe, "Here I was thinking you have an intelligent mind and a golden heart. But you have such a sexy body too."

Ritvik swooped down on her, crushing her mouth with his, his hands pushing her top up to caress her waist.

The next minute, they were tearing at each other's clothes, throwing the garments helter skelter as they fell on each other. Ritvik had not been with a woman in over three years and this was the first time he really felt attracted to one in all that while. For Sia, well, she didn't want to dwell too much on it. She was no virgin but she had never wanted to be with a man the way she wanted to make love with Ritvik.

Her hands caressed his wide shoulders even as Ritvik kissed his way down her neck to the top of her breasts, making her jump off the bed. All the nerves in her body came alive as he nipped and stroked her erogenous zones just above her areola. Sia mewled when she felt his damp tongue skimming over a turgid nipple, wanting more. "Ritvik." She held his head close to her breast, pressing her body upwards and gave a deep sigh when she felt his mouth close over the tip as he sucked on it gently. "Oh yes!" she moaned in response, her fingers digging into his scalp.

Ritvik cupped her right breast in his left hand, his thumb stroking over the areola in a circular motion, making her buck in his arms. His right hand caressed her from shoulder to waist to hip to thigh, driving her nuts. He lifted his head to blow gently over the wet tip of the breast he had been suckling, watching it pucker. With a wicked grin on his face, Ritvik bent down to take a bite, making Sia moan louder than before.

He turned to give his attention to the other breast, squeezing it gently with his hand while brushing his tongue over the tip, making Sia thrash her legs under him in response.

"Ritvik, that feels so good," she groaned, her arms tightly wound around his neck, even as she wrapped a leg around his middle.

"You have a wonderful body, honey," he spoke in a whisper, his charcoal gaze burning into hers. "I love the shape of your breasts. They are perfect."

Sia was turned on like she never was before, his words, along with his caresses, arousing her to fever pitch. She pushed him on the bed to climb over him to sit on his flat stomach.

Amused, Ritvik looked at her, his hands at her waist, asking, "What are you going to do?"

"I want to have my way with you now."

"Okay..." He caressed her with his eyes, watching the colour rush up her skin. Tight curls of hair danced around her cheeks as with a determined expression on her face, Sia bent down to kiss him on his lips. Ritvik choked when he felt her lush breasts pressing into his chest, making his shaft twitch in response. His hands ran down her silky back before settling down on her bottom as he kneaded the shapely curves. She was so soft and luscious, all woman. He groaned loudly when he felt her teeth nipping his flat male nipple. "Vixen."

Sia giggled, rubbing her tongue over the area. "There, I kissed it alright."

"Oh yeah!"

She shimmied her way down his body, making him painfully hard as she settled down on his thighs to take his shaft in both her hands. "You are huge," she declared, stroking him with her hands before flicking her tongue over the tip.

"Sia!" Ritvik moved then, too impatient with the need to bury himself inside her. He pushed her on the bed and removing the condom which he had carried in his jeans pocket, rolled it on in a hurry before entering her core, which was invitingly wet. He settled within her with a grunt, wrapping her legs around his waist. "Are you okay?" he asked Sia as her eyes were tightly shut.

Sia opened slumberous silver-grey eyes to look into his questioning gaze. "Never better," she smiled.

Ritvik pressed his lips to hers, his tongue pushing within as he began the age-old rhythm when he pumped into her, first slowly, then gaining momentum as they both lost control, giving themselves up to their bodies' whims. An orgasm ripped through Sia, making her moan his name repeatedly, tears pouring down the sides of her face.

Ritvik groaned in turn, calling out to Sia as he came a few seconds later, as he had never come before. He fell against her, exhausted. Moving to the side so as to not crush her, Ritvik pulled the comforter over them even as he held her close to his chest. And that's how they went to sleep, spooned against each other.

14

Sia was truly excited about the hot affair she was having with her boss. It was obviously the best phase of her life. The casualness of it was what was appealing, no rules to take away from the joy of it. When they were at work, they were professionals; she never deviated from her role as salon manager and gave him his due as the CEO of the organisation which ran Cleopatra's. But in bed, they were equals. The secret looks they shared when no one was looking were the best. And then there were the naughty WhatsApp messages from Ritvik which Sia found irresistible.

Ritvik insisted on having a weekly head massage at the salon. The sessions were such fun and the height of titillation. Their lovemaking on those nights was more uninhibited than the others, while the body massages that he gave her in the underground bedroom were erotic and Sia revelled in those. Though Ritvik insisted that he was the one who was having the most fun, getting to touch and pet every inch of her luscious body.

It was two weeks after they had become lovers when Sia opened her phone as she had a half an hour break before her next client. There was a message from Ritvik, saying, "Meet me for five mins? Now? My office." Sia noticed that it had come ten minutes ago.

Wondering about the urgency, Sia told Andy that she would be back shortly before she left for Ritvik's office. She knocked before walking in to see Akhil sitting with their boss. "I'm sorry. I'll come later."

Ritvik's voice stopped her when she would have turned away. "Wait Sia. I'm almost done with Akhil. I'll be with you in a few minutes."

Sia sat down on the chair next to Akhil, silently watching the two men at work. Her eyes kept straying to Ritvik, her gaze admiring his handsome features. He looked delectable in a three-piece suit in jet black with a maroon tie. All she wanted to do was tear the clothes off him and have her way with him. Ritvik's eyes flashed to hers for a split second as if he could read her thoughts before he turned his attention to what Akhil was saying. Colour rushed up Sia's cheeks when she caught the desire burning in his black gaze.

Akhil got up after five minutes to shake Ritvik's hand. "Okay boss. I don't think there should be any issues. Please convey my best wishes to both Rohit and Tasha and love to their newborn."

"I will. Be seeing you soon buddy."

Ritvik got up to walk towards Sia once Akhil left the cabin. He pulled her into his arms to give her a brief, but hard kiss. "Honey, I'm off to Mumbai for a few days. My brother's wife has delivered a baby boy this morning."

"Congratulations, Uncle Ritvik," said Sia, kissing him on his cheek. "You enjoy yourself."

"I'm sure I will, though I'm going to miss you terribly." Ritvik buried his face in her neck, nuzzling her. He hadn't given it a thought until just now but it was going to be a wrench leaving her.

Sia kissed him on his mouth, patting his cheek. "Just a few days, right? Come back fast. I'm going nowhere."

"Do you want to come with me?" Ritvik's hands were splayed on her bottom as he pressed her pelvis to his aroused manhood.

Sia laughed, shaking her head. "I know I have contacts in high places at my place of work, but I draw the line at asking favours. It's been barely a month since I took up this job."

"You know something?" Ritvik whispered suggestively into her ear as he drew a damp tongue over the shape, "Your contacts in lower places might work better." He took her hand and placed it against the bulge in his pants.

Sia laughed as colour seeped into her cheeks. "So, when are you leaving? Do we have a few minutes?"

"A few minutes?"

Sia nodded, giving him a saucy look. "I've been fantasising about having my way with you across your antique rosewood desk. What say?"

Ritvik lifted his head to look down at her, a wide grin on his face. "I just love it when you get all innovative."

Ritvik, Aarya and Meera took off to Mumbai by his private jet a couple of hours later. Aarya was used to a bit of travelling by now and enjoyed herself, checking out the clouds. Father and daughter also had a wonderful time as Ritvik read to her from an Amar Chitra Katha comic on Lord Ganesha.

After the story got over, she bombarded him with more questions about her newborn cousin. "I wanna see cuthe baby. Whath is baby name?"

"We will find out when we get there," Ritvik answered patiently, as he held her on his lap. He knew that Rohit and Tasha had been toying with a choice between Aahan and Mehul if it was going to be a boy.

He had encouraged Meera Aunty to take a break while he spent time with little Aarya. "How big is baby?"

"He must be small, about this size." Ritvik showed her his forearm.

Aarya giggled. "Small baby."

"Yes."

"I wanna see. Can we thake baby home?"

Ritvik laughed as he ruffled her hair affectionately. "The baby will want his mummy and daddy. He will cry if we take him away. Maybe some months later, we can ask Rohit *Chacha* and Tasha *Chachi* to bring the baby home. Would you like that?"

"Whath is mummy?" Aarya asked her father curiously. She had never heard the word before now.

"Rohit *Chacha* is the baby's daddy, right?" Aarya nodded her head vigorously. "Tasha *Chachi* is baby's mummy."

"Who is Aarya's mummy?" Her little hand opened wide in a questioning gesture, as she looked at her father's face innocently.

"Hey, look down at that." Ritvik pointed through the window, as he decided that the best course of action would be to distract his daughter rather than tell her lies. It wasn't possible anyway to explain the meaning of surrogacy to his child and he didn't want to tell her that she had no mother. Which somehow didn't seem very fair.

"Whath?" Childlike, Aarya forgot her question as she pressed her nose to the window, her mouth opening wide as she looked down at the buildings which seemed to come closer and closer as the plane approached Mumbai airport. She clapped her hands gleefully. "I'm goin' to see baby."

Ritvik held her, wondering at how Sia's face had flashed before his mind's eye when Aarya had asked about her mummy.

It was seven when father and daughter walked into the private nursing home where Tasha had delivered her son. Rohit met them at the entrance. "Aarya, sweetheart." He lifted his niece into his arms, giving her a kiss. Aarya touched her uncle's smooth, cleanshaven cheek and gave him a wet kiss. "I wanna see baby. Whath is baby name?"

Rohit laughed. "Sure, sweetheart. Baby is Aarya's little brother and his name is Mehul."

"Me'ul." Aarya clapped her hands, sliding out of Rohit's arms. "I wanna see."

"In a minute, sweetie," said Ritvik, hugging his brother. "Congrats bro! How's Tasha?"

"She's fine now." Rohit grimaced.

"Tough?" Ritvik commiserated, even as a sudden thought struck him. He had never bothered to find out what the surrogate mother must have undergone while giving birth to his child.

"Tasha insists it was tougher on me since I was helpless. She seems okay now. But *yaar*, I don't think I want her to undergo the pain ever again."

Ritvik hugged Rohit again. "Can we see them now?"

"Of course, come along. Mamma and Pappa left only half an hour back to go home to my apartment." Rohit turned left to walk down a corridor to reach a luxurious suite. Rhea and Jamie were coming over the next day.

"Hey Ritvik, Aarya." Tasha called out from her cot.

Seeing her lying on a bed, Aarya ran up to Tasha and asked, "*Chachi* noth well?" She pulled Tasha's hand to kiss it.

Tasha laughed, bending down to kiss Aarya's forehead. "No darling. I'm fine. You want to see your little brother?"

"Yeth." Aarya jumped from one foot to the other, totally excited.

"Come here, sweetheart." Rohit called his niece over to the cradle which was placed on the other side of Tasha's bed.

Ritvik gave Tasha a hug. "Congrats, new mom. How are you feeling? Rohit says you had a difficult time." He kissed her on her forehead.

"I feel awesome now that the baby's out." Tasha grinned. "Yeah, it was a bit rough, but nothing which I couldn't take." She lowered her voice to say, "But Rohit was rather shaken."

"I'm sure. He must have felt helpless watching you in pain."

Aarya held the railing as she peeped inside and was startled to see the crumpled red face of the baby who was fast asleep. "Me'ul," she called out to him.

"Mehul is sleeping, sweetie. Let's not disturb him," said Ritvik as he looked down at his nephew, touching a gentle finger to the baby's forehead.

"I wanna thouch."

Mehul screwed up his face, stretching his little body.

"Me'ul awake, Daddhie," said Aarya. "Can I thouch?"

"Of course, Aarya. Here, let me get him out of his cradle," said Rohit, lifting his waking son out. He sat on the couch nearby, holding the baby in his arms for Aarya to see and touch.

She touched the baby's hand, giggling at her uncle. "Softh."

"May I?" Ritvik took Mehul in his arms, tucking him close to his heart. "He looks exactly like you, Rohit."

"That's what I've been telling him," said Tasha, laughing.

It was more than half an hour before Ritvik persuaded an extremely reluctant Aarya to leave. "We'll come back tomorrow morning."

"I wanna sthay with baby, pleathe Rohith *Chacha*." Aarya appealed to her uncle.

Rohit swept the little girl into his arms. "*Daada* and *Daadi* are waiting for you at home, sweetheart. Don't you want to see them?"

"Yeth." Aarya nodded her head vigorously.

"Tell you what? You go with your Daddy and meet *Daada* and *Daadi*. Then come back in the morning. Okay?"

"Okay." She gave him another kiss, touching his cheek again. "Bye *chacha*, bye *chachi*, bye Me'ul." She jumped into Ritvik's arms, throwing her own around his neck. "Leth's go, Daddhie."

Ritvik laughed, "Of course, my little imp. Bye bro. I'll see you tomorrow. And Tasha, you take care."

"Daddhie, say 'bye' to Me'ul."

"Bye Mehul," Ritvik called out, blowing a kiss in the newborn's direction before stepping out of the suite, carrying Aarya in his arms.

Alok and Menaka pampered their granddaughter as Aarya chattered non-stop, telling them about the new baby. She insisted on sleeping with her *Daadi* and had her way.

Ritvik left along with her and Meera Aunty the next evening, after promising to bring Aarya back to meet her little brother again soon.

15

"Hey." Sia's heart went banging against her chest when she lifted the phone to hear Ritvik's familiar voice, waking her up completely.

"Ritvik! Where are you?" Sia sat up against her bed head to switch on the table lamp.

"Are you home?"

"Where else?" Sia smiled to herself.

"Will you open the door?"

Sia squealed delightedly, disconnecting the call and leaving her phone on the side table before rushing to the door. Opening it, she fell into Ritvik's arms, burying her face in his chest. "Welcome back."

Ritvik was floored by her more than enthusiastic greeting as he walked into her apartment, half carrying her. "Missed you, honey."

She kissed him on his lips before saying, "I missed you too."

"Let me see what you're wearing." Ritvik moved Sia a couple of inches away from him to look down at her. His jet-black eyes glowed with desire when he saw that she wore no bra under her fire engine red nightshirt, her stiff nipples thrust out invitingly. Cupping his right hand over her left breast, he groaned, "You look sexy," before placing his lips on hers and kissing her deeply.

Sia pressed closer even as his left hand moved down to caress her bare bottom. She swung a leg around his hip, holding on tightly to his neck with both her arms. "So do you."

"What's this?" Ritvik fingered the undergarment which covered her feminine core.

"It's a thong."

"Now this I must see." He lifted her and took her to bed. Sitting down, he sat her on his lap, her back pressed to his chest. Cupping both her breasts, he kneaded the tips between his thumbs and index fingers, making her moan with want. His teeth grazed against her collarbone, as her head tilted back against his shoulder. With one clean sweep, Ritvik removed the nightshirt off her. His eyes narrowed and then went wide when he saw the lacy red thong which covered her privates. "Sia..." He cupped his right hand against her vagina, moving it slowly up and down, even as his left arm crushed her breasts as he held her close to his chest. "I want you."

Sia turned sideways to kiss one corner of his mouth before tilting her head to look deeply into his blazing dark eyes, her own grey gaze smokier than ever. "So take me." She quickly opened the buttons of his shirt, pushing it out of the way to explore his hair roughened chest. She fell back on her bed, pulling him down along with her, taking a bite into his shoulder.

With a groan, Ritvik got up to pull off his pants and briefs before lying next to her. He kissed her on the lips first, his tongue exploring every corner of her mouth, taking his own sweet time as he revelled in the taste. He moved further down, drawing his damp tongue down her chin, her neck and then to the top of her breasts. He paused before tracing circles around the areola with his tongue, making Sia pant hard.

She held his head between her hands as he made love to her breasts. Moaning again, she called out, "Ritvik, please."

He lifted his head to look at her, a sexy smile on his face. "Please what?"

"I..." She placed her index finger on his lips, tracing the shape. "I want your mouth..." Her throat choked even as her cheeks grew hot when he sucked gently on her finger after drawing it deeply inside his mouth. She couldn't believe that it could be as erotic as feeling him suckling her breast.

"You were saying..." A black eyebrow rose up to touch his hairline as Ritvik gave her a wicked grin.

Sia placed her still damp finger on the tip of her breast before saying, "I want your mouth here."

Ritvik bent down and drew his tongue across the nipple, his gaze still locked with hers.

"Oh yes, I like that." Sia moaned, her eyes growing heavy.

He drew the tip into his mouth and suckled slowly and deeply, making her jump off the bed. Turning his head, he gave the same attention to the other breast before kissing his way down, his beard brushing against her body, making her sensitive skin scream out for more.

Sia thrashed her legs, trying to hold him close. Only, Ritvik spread her legs wide and settled on his knees in between, eyeing the sexy red lace that was barely there, the only garment which covered her. With gentle hands on both sides of her body, Ritvik pulled the scrap of lace down, inch by torturous inch, his breath coming out in soft gasps as he eyed the treasure being revealed in front of his avid gaze. The black curls protecting her feminine mound were tighter than the cork screw curls on her head. Pulling the thong slowly down her legs, Ritvik took it off to throw it down on the floor to join the rest of their clothes.

Sia stared at Ritvik, curiosity and desire warring within her as she wondered what he planned to do now that he had her completely naked in front of him. Expecting to feel his hand against her vagina, she gasped in shock when he bent down to place his mouth at the entrance, even as he held her thighs firmly in his large hands. "Ritvik! What are you doing?"

He didn't reply as he ran his tongue slowly down the vertical seam, before pressing down with his hands on her thighs, driving Sia crazy as he made love to her core, his lips and tongue and teeth relentless in their giving of pleasure. She thrashed on the bed, her hands in Ritvik's hair as she pulled it out of its knot, her fingers tangled in it. It wasn't long before Sia groaned long and loud as an explosive orgasm ripped through her, her eyes tearing up in emotion. She had never experienced such intense pleasure ever before.

She didn't realise she had spoken out loud until she heard Ritvik saying, "Neither have I."

He lifted his head and went to lie next to her, his throbbing manhood pressed against her thigh. "Sia." He kissed her on her lips, his hands pulling her close to his manly chest. "You taste delicious."

She buried her red face in his neck, not really able to look into his eyes as she felt shy all of a sudden. Recovering soon, she realised that he had made her reach her climax, so unselfishly, not having found satisfaction for himself.

"Ritvik." Sia pushed him down on the bed, kissing him on his lips. She sat on his stomach, admiring his looks as she watched his long hair spread out on her pillow, his black gaze slumberous as he looked back at her. When he placed his hands on her waist, Sia protested, "No. I want you to relax. Let me make love to you."

Amusement danced in his eyes as he looked at her determined expression. He lifted his hands off her waist at her behest, only to skim the backs over her breasts, making her protest loudly. "What?" He grinned mischievously, turning his hands to squeeze the twin mounds. "I like touching you, you know. You are perfectly shaped, soft and springy as well. I..."

Sia slapped his hands away. "I'm not a soft toy." She gave him a fake glare.

Ritvik laughed, shaking his head, but refusing to let go. "That you're not. A soft toy doesn't have a crazy pulse rate." He let go of her left breast to place a finger at her neck. "Oops! Just feel that."

"Ritvik." She held his manly wrists in her hands. "Are you going to keep your hands to yourself?" She wiggled her bottom over his manhood, making him harder than ever, before lying down on his chest. "Forget it." She shut her eyes, pretending not to care, doing her best to clamp down on the giggle which was desperate to escape her throat.

"Hey! Why did you stop?" Ritvik shoved a hand into her hair to lift her head up.

Sia shrugged, her breasts bouncing provocatively. "Since you don't seem really interested..." She pouted, drawing his glance to lips which were swollen from his kisses.

"Says who?" Ritvik's voice was a feral growl. "Get on with it, woman. Just don't forget that my shaft has been burning to be buried inside you for such a long time now." His voice was thick with unbridled passion as he removed his hands off her to place them under his head.

Sia skimmed her hands over his hair roughened chest, before bending down to kiss him all over, her wet tongue playing havoc with his libido.

"Sia..." he groaned.

She raked her nails over his thighs, before pressing her cheek to his pubis, making mewling sounds as she rubbed her face against him. Taking his shaft in her hands, she caressed him from the root to the tip, making him twitch.

Before Sia realised what he was about, Ritvik lifted her by the waist and brought her down against his rock-hard manhood, grunting with pleasure. Sia moaned as she felt him filling her before she splayed her hands on his chest and rode him, hard and fast, her heart galloping at record speed, her head thrown back as her hips ground into his.

Ritvik squeezed her breasts in his hands, savouring their firmness in his palms before an orgasm— the most powerful he had ever had—tore through him.

She flopped against his chest, totally spent, and went to sleep almost immediately.

Sia woke up in the morning to find herself alone in bed. Before the feeling of disappointment could take over, she noticed two red roses on the bedside table, tucked into a glass vase. She was thrilled to notice that they were damp with dew, obviously having been plucked afresh. She pressed her lips to them in turn, the red glow of the flowers spreading to her cheeks as she recalled the previous night's lovemaking.

Ritvik did seem to bring out the wanton in her! Not that she minded, not at all. Sia's whole body thrummed with excitement at the thought of coming face to face with him today.

16

Indrajeet and Rajvardhan Thakore arrived home for a ten-day break. Their mother Ragini was so happy to see her sons that tears shimmered in her eyes. "Our home hasn't been the same with both of you gone." Indrajeet had left to study abroad three years ago while it had been a year since Rajvardhan had also joined the Harvard Business School. And as for home, as Ragini called it, it was actually a palace. Shabby it might be, but it was still a fabulous structure contructed of stone with more than four hundred rooms built on two levels.

Indrajeet hugged their mother while Rajvardhan tweaked their younger sister Dayanita's ear. "So, what mischief have you been up to, Nita?" asked Rajvardhan, grinning at his sister. She looked lovelier than ever.

Dayanita shrugged. "Nothing *yaar*, Raj. So, what have you got for me, Jeet?" She queried of her eldest brother.

"Why, nothing of course. Have you forgotten that we're still students living on a shoestring budget?" Rajvardhan couldn't resist teasing his sister. "Tell me something, has the illustrious Ritvik Bansal popped the question yet?"

Dayanita made a face at Rajvardhan. With barely a couple of years of difference in their ages, the younger siblings bickered almost always.

Gajendar walked into the palace just then, a wide smile of welcome on his face. He hugged his strapping sons in turn. "Glad to see you boys. So how is it going?"

Indrajeet chatted with his father while Rajvardhan and Dayanita walked into Santhini Devi's quarters. "Grandma, see who has come."

"Hey Granny, how have you been?"

"I'm fine, Rajvardhan." The old lady patted his head in blessing as Rajvardhan bent down to touch her feet. "Are you enjoying yourself at Harvard University?"

Rajvardhan grimaced even as his eyes danced with mischief. "What enjoyment Granny! My nose is forever stuck to the grind as I work twenty-five hours in a day." He groaned dramatically, sitting down next to the matriarch. "You tell me how you've been. Are your old bones all in working condition?"

Santhini looked at her younger grandson who looked exactly like how his grandfather—her husband—used to be. But Rajvardhan treated his grandmother like a naughty child, talking to her like an equal, without showing her the respect she felt was her due. She wasn't sure if she liked his irreverent attitude. But then, that's how Rajvardhan was. "You'll find out when you are my age," she declared in response to his question.

Rajvardhan shook his head. "No way. I don't plan to be as unfit as you are, Granny. You sit around gossiping all your waking hours. No wonder you've become fatter than you were last year." And that was so true! At sixty-five, Santhini Devi was a couch potato. She still considered herself a queen and insisted on being waited upon hand and foot. She kept a large brass bell next to her always. It was probably only her right hand which got any exercise at all as she lifted the bell to ring it about twenty-five times in a day.

Neither Indrajeet nor Rajvardhan cared much for their grandmother's attitude. While Indrajeet was too polite to say much, Rajvardhan had no such qualms. Their indifference sprung from the fact that Santhini Devi treated their mother Ragini miserably.

"Where's Indrajeet? Why don't you go away and send him to me?" Santhini glared at her younger grandson.

"Nita, go get Jeet. Tell him Granny wants to meet him." Rajvardhan lolled back on his grandmother's bed, irritating her even further.

Dayanita left the romm promptly to find Indrajeet who was chatting with their father. "Jeet, Grandma wants to meet you."

Indrajeet got up to hug his sister, saying, "You tell her that she's in queue and will have to wait." He winked. "You never did ask me what I've got for you from the US of A."

Dayanita squealed with joy. "I asked you, only you were busy talking to Dad. And Raj said... I'm going to kill him. So, what did you get for me?"

"You'll find a red suitcase amongst my luggage. It's all yours." Indrajeet patted his little sister's cheek. "Hey, and I hope you've stopped chasing poor Ritvik. Give the man a break!" He called out to his sister who was already halfway up the staircase at the other end of the hall.

"Double murder it will have to be." Dayanita yelled at him over her shoulder as she continued on her way.

Dinner was a cheerful affair as the six of them sat around the table, eating their way through a seven-course meal. "Mom, I need to cycle for twenty km at least, to get this worked out of my system," groaned Rajvardhan, rubbing a large hand over his flat stomach.

"You are mad," declared Santhini Devi, glaring at Rajvardhan. "Why don't you go riding on a horse instead of a stupid cycle?"

Rajvardhan laughed. "Granny, I need the exercise, not the horse."

Gajendar roared with laughter, refusing to shut up when his mother turned her furious gaze on him.

Indrajeet got up. "I'm going for a walk. Do you want to go with me, Mamma?"

"Why don't you call her Mom like the others do?" It was Indrajeet's turn to be scolded.

"That's because Mamma prefers to be addressed that way." Indrajeet hugged his mother, bending down to kiss the top of her head. "Go with me?"

"I need to clear the table and get things done for the night. I..."

"We have enough people to do all that, Mamma. I'm sure Pappa can supervise that or even Grandma. You come along with me." He refused to take 'no' for an answer as he dragged his mother out into the garden which was the only thing which was properly maintained in their home, all thanks to Gajendar's green fingers.

The aroma of jasmine greeted them as mother and son walked out onto the portico and took a right turn, Indrajeet's arm around Ragini's shoulders.

"Mamma, have you thought about encouraging Nita to study further? Or is getting married her only aim in life?" There was a small frown on Indrajeet's face as he spoke to his mother. "She's barely twenty. What's the hurry to get hitched?" Indrajeet knew that his father wasn't for the idea of marriage. But then, Dayanita had flatly refused their father's offer of sending her abroad for further studies.

Ragini stopped in her tracks to look up at her son who towered head and shoulders above her five-and-a-half-foot height. "I don't mind either way. But you know Nita listens only to your grandmother and is convinced she should make Ritvik Bansal fall for her. Your grandmother says, he's so rich that he can set right all our financial problems."

Indrajeet held his mother's hand and gently pulled her into walking again, continuing to talk. "What financial problems, Mamma? Ritvik paid us for our summer palace and now we have a lot of money, with all our loans paid off. I should be completing my studies this year, and you know I'm also working and earning really well. We don't need a rich husband for Nita to set right our non-existent problems. I don't like this idea of her chasing the poor man. If he liked her, he'd have said so by now, right?"

Ragini nodded her head slowly, accepting her firstborn's logic. "So, what do you suggest?"

"We need to make Nita understand that she's too young to get married. She can study or she can even go to work..."

"Work? Are you mad, Jeet? We can't send our womenfolk to work. Your grandmother will be scandalised." Ragini told him in a shocked voice.

Indrajeet laughed. "I'm not asking about Grandma's opinion, Mamma. She's still living in the British era and seems to be unaware that it has been seventy years since they left our country. I am asking you about your opinion. An idle mind is the devil's workshop and we can see that only too well when we look at Grandma. You, Mamma, are busy managing our home and servants and have not a single moment to sit. But Nita, what the hell does she do all day long?"

Ragini gave a deep sigh. "I have stopped interfering, Jeet. It doesn't make sense if both of us, your grandmother and I, fight over her like two dogs over a single piece of bone." Her voice was bitter. Santhini Devi insisted on Dayanita growing up to be in her own image. While Ragini didn't like or approve of this, she didn't have much of a choice but to stand back and watch. The situation was a bit too complicated and she didn't want to bother her husband regarding the same.

"I understand. I've already spoken to Pappa. I'll handle Nita. I just wanted to know that you wouldn't mind."

"Not at all! I know you want the best for your sister." Maybe because he had grown up in a royal household which had no cash to fulfil every whim, Indrajeet had grown up fast, taking his responsibilities a mite too seriously. At twenty-five, he was ready to take care of his family and maybe the princely genes had also contributed to it.

"And how's your health? I hope you're taking care of yourself..." Mother and son took a turn around the garden, continuing to chat about everything under the sun.

It was only the next day when Santhini Devi could get a private word with her eldest grandchild. "Indrajeet, listen. You know I've been trying to get Dayanita married off to Ritvik Bansal..."

Indrajeet sighed loudly. "Grandma, does it even strike you that the man might not be interested? He's thirty-one to Nita's twenty. What's the point?" His voice was mild. He had learned early on in life that it never made sense to fight his grandmother, not if he wanted to get his own way.

"What does that matter? Your grandfather was twelve years older than me. Didn't we have a wonderful life?"

Though he had never met his grandfather, Indrajeet could still commiserate with the man who had been married to the tyrant of a woman who wanted to run everyone's life. "I'm sure you did. But then, you also got married when you were sixteen. Which is illegal nowadays."

"That really doesn't matter since Dayanita is twenty. Now stop arguing and listen to me. Your sister refuses to go to Ritvik's hotel because there's this new employee at the beauty salon who has insulted her. Then there's the issue of Ritvik's daughter. You know Dayanita hates children. I..."

Indrajeet threw his hands up in the air. "What crap are you talking about? Aren't Ritvik's employees his business? How can Nita interfere? And why would Ritvik care if Nita likes or hates his daughter? The child is no one else's business but his own. Let me talk to Nita..."

"Indrajeet!" Santhini Devi gave him a quelling look. "Will you stop interrupting me? There's a plan I want to discuss with you." No, she would never admit, not in words, that she needed his help. Lesser the number of others who got to know about her plan, the better.

"Go on." Indrajeet presented an expressionless face to his grandmother, even though he wanted to give her a shouting. But Dayanita wasn't going to escape getting a piece of his mind, not this time. All this long, Dayanita running after Bansal had been a standing joke in the family. But it wasn't funny any longer.

"Only something drastic will bring that man to his senses. He..."

"Are you saying Ritvik isn't in his senses?" Indrajeet couldn't help interrupting his grandmother, his tongue tucked firmly in cheek. He was rather fed up of the topic by now.

Santhini Devi shook her walking stick at her grown-up grandson. "I told you not to interrupt. Just keep quiet for a while and listen. I have a splendid plan. As I was saying, this is something drastic, but it will definitely work. Let's pretend to kidnap Bansal's daughter..."

Indrajeet got up from his chair, towering menacingly over his grandmother. "You are my grandmother; which is the only reason I am not turning you over to the police. Just wipe this idea off your dirty mind this very second. But Pappa will definitely get to know about this. And if, by any chance, I find out that Nita is involved in this plan, I'm going to beat the daylights out of her and make sure she never spends any time alone with you, ever."

Santhini Devi stared in awe at Indrajeet. Instead of getting angry at the lack of respect in his voice and stance, she was truly impressed with his behaviour. She had always been under the impression that he was mild, insipid actually, like his mother. But just now, he had proved that the Thakore royal blood ran in his veins. While he resembled his mother strongly, she couldn't help but notice the Thakore nose and cleft in his chin. But it was the expression in his fiery brown eyes which appeared priceless to the old matriarch. "Sit down, Indrajeet, and don't forget that you're speaking to your grandmother, who also happens to be a queen. Alright, so you don't like the idea. Come up with a better one. I am getting old and I want to see our home, this palace, restored to its former glory."

"Wouldn't it make better sense to make your grown-up grandsons go to work and earn the money for it, instead of selling your granddaughter to the highest bidder?" Indrajeet refused to sit down, pacing up and down his grandmother's room. He could accept that she wanted the palace to look rich again. So did he! But it was her methods which he objected to. He suddenly went on his knees before his grandmother. "Tell you what? I'll make you a promise to restore our home within two years from today. In return, I want your promise that you will not run Nita's life. Agreed?"

Santhini Devi glared at him. "You are trying to remove the very purpose of my life..."

"What purpose? Of killing all chances of Nita leading a happy life, ever? Get a life, Grandma."

"How dare you? Don't forget..."

"...that you are the Thakore queen in a country which has been a republic for the last seven decades. I haven't forgotten that. That still doesn't give you the right to spoil Nita's life."

"I knew it. I just knew it when that mother of yours dragged you out for a walk yesterday. I knew she would poison you, my own flesh and blood, against me." Her voice rose with her temper.

Indrajeet laughed, still on his knees beside her. "You are crazy. It was I who took Mamma for a walk. And you very well know that. You want me to take you for a walk? Come along then. There's no need to feel jealous."

"Why should I feel jealous of your mother?" Santhini Devi was tempted to call her daughter-in-law all kinds of abusive names. She also knew that Indrajeet would never tolerate it.

"Tell you what? There's a new club which has come up and only rich, elderly people from ex-royal families have entry to it. Do you want to become a member? It will give you a new purpose in life."

Santhini Devi's old eyes lit up. She had also heard about it. But the membership fees were huge. Her lips drooped as a shadow crossed over her face. "Forget it. We can't afford it."

"Says who?" Indrajeet looked up at the creased old face with love in his own. Placing his hands on the arms of her sofa, he leaned closer. "You have a grandson who makes a lot of money. I can easily purchase a membership for you. Just tell me the word."

"You can?" Her eyes lit up again. "But what about the renovations for our home? You'll need the money for it."

Indrajeet shook his head. "I have both issues covered. You'll have our home looking amazing in two years. In the meanwhile, I want you to improve your health at the club while you enjoy yourself with your old friends. But before that, I want your promise."

"What promise?" The matriarch gave him a wily look from under her greying lashes, her gaze sharp as a knife.

Her grandson laughed. "You know what I'm talking about, Grandma mine." Indrajeet put out a hand, palm up, "Your promise not to run Dayanita's life."

Santhini Devi sighed. She knew when she was defeated. But then, her grandson had just offered her a piece of heaven. She placed her wrinkled palm over his, saying, "I promise."

"That's my girl." Indrajeet got up to kiss her cheek. "I'm off to the club right now. Do you want to go with me?"

She nodded eagerly, getting up from her recliner.

Indrajeet Thakore was terribly disturbed when he got to know two days later that Aarya Bansal had been kidnapped. His grandmother, Rajmata Santhini Devi, had gone back on her word.

17

It was time to introduce Sia and Aarya. Ritvik had come to that decision the moment he woke up in Sia's arms. His head had been buried against her breasts; his arm wrapped around her slim waist. She was growing on him, and speedily too.

He had dressed himself noiselessly, keen not to disturb her. Though he still wasn't sure how he had resisted kissing her. Going down the stairs, his eyes fell on the roses which grew abundantly in the garden. Breaking a couple of red ones along with their long stalks, he had gone back to her apartment and entered it silently, using his master key. Placing them in a vase, he had left the roses near her bed, sure that she would get his message.

It was around four in the evening when father and daughter arrived at the back of the hotel's garden to play with a large rubber ball. Anyone stepping out of Cleopatra's would be able to see them. Aarya was excited as she ran around the garden chasing the ball, catching it and throwing it in different directions. She clapped her hands, laughing, when Ritvik feigned not to be able to catch the ball as he ran after it.

Noticing the father-daughter duo playing in the garden, Asha went back inside to tell Sia about it. The moment Sia was free, she stepped out to see for herself. Wondering who the little girl was—no, Ritvik hadn't spoken to her about her—Sia walked over to them with a smile on her face.

Ritvik stopped playing when he saw Sia coming towards them, a wide smile on his face as he held his daughter's hand. "Hello Sia. Meet my daughter Aarya.

Ritvik had a daughter who appeared to be about two or maybe three years old.

Sia stared at the little girl when she was at a distance of a couple of feet from them. Why was Aarya's face so familiar? She had seen the little girl's face, not just once, but many times. But then, Sia had never even known that Ritvik had a daughter, let alone met her. A deep frown settled on her face as she noticed the contradictory thoughts which chased one after the other through her mind. Could it be...? Suddenly, light dawned on Sia's face before horror struck, her heart feeling as if it was being crushed by a giant hand. Her head whirled, her breath coming in gasps as Sia blacked out for the first time in her life, completely unaware that she had crumpled on the grass before Ritvik could catch her.

Ritvik was shocked out of his wits as he rushed to Sia, going down on his knees beside her. One minute she had been walking in his direction with a smile on her face. The next, her face had turned a deathly pallor before she fell down. Had she suffered from a heart attack? He refused to believe it as he lifted her head on to his lap. It must have been a shock to find out that he had a daughter; that must be it, he decided. He had been stupid not to mention Aarya to Sia before. For all he knew, she must have presumed that he had Aarya's mother hidden somewhere. No wonder she had collapsed at his feet.

"Get your water bottle, sweetie," he told his hovering daughter.

"Whath happened, Daddhie?" Aarya looked a bit sad, unsure of what was happening, even while she picked up the tension in her father.

Ritvik hugged his daughter, giving her a kiss, saying, "Nothing serious, sweetie. I think Sia Aunty forgot to eat lunch." He gave his daughter a weak smile, even as his hand felt for the pulse at Sia's neck, relieved to find it beating, though erratically.

"Oh!" Satisfied with his answer, Aarya rushed over to the other end of the garden to bring back the water bottle which they had brought along with them.

Ritvik poured some water in his hands and gently sprinkled it over Sia's face. Relieved to see her eyes opening, though in a slit, he raised her head a few inches, placing the mouth of the water bottle against her lips. "Don't get up yet, Sia. Drink some water."

Sia took a sip before pushing the bottle away. She got up to sit down on the grass, staring at the little girl next to Ritvik in morbid fascination.

"You no eath lunch?" Aarya asked Sia innocently, a smile on her little face.

Sia's expression was bewildered as she looked questioningly at Ritvik.

He gave her a weak smile, saying, "Aarya got scared when you fainted. I told her that you must have missed your lunch." His eyes warned her not to contradict him.

Sia got up to stand, dusting her pants. "Yeah, that's what I did." Her throat was parched while her face was pinched.

Ritvik wanted to explain to Sia the circumstances of Aarya's birth, but not in his daughter's hearing.

Before he could say anything, Aarya piped up, "You should eath lunch. Come home. Meera Aunthie will make sandhwich." She took Sia's hand in hers, pulling at it.

It was a wonder how Sia held back the tears which rushed into her eyes when she felt the small hand in hers. She brushed back the cork screw curls which fell on the little forehead, bending down to press her lips to the top of Aarya's head. "It's alright, darling. I need to get back to work."

Ritvik cursed himself, swearing under his breath. He was worried that Sia might just disappear if he let her go now without an explanation. "Sia, listen. Come home. Meera Aunty will fix you a sandwich indeed." He picked up the ball, water bottle and towel as he escorted Sia and Aarya to the King of Spades suite on the third floor which was their home.

Aarya's non-stop chatter seemed to underline the silence between the two adults. Ritvik tried to catch Sia's eye, only she refused to take them off his daughter, even as she wouldn't let go of Aarya's hand. Not that the little girl seemed to mind.

Sia managed to swallow a quarter of the cheese sandwich under Aarya's vigilant gaze, taking gulps of the coffee which helped her swallow the food which kept getting stuck in her choking throat.

"Meera Aunty, could you please give Aarya a bath?" Ritvik requested the older woman.

"Come Aarya."

"I wanna be with Sia Aunthie." Aarya protested.

"Come on sweetie. Sia's going to spend the evening with us." He had called the salon to tell them that she wouldn't be going back for the rest of the day. "You go have a bath and come back."

Aarya looked at Sia as if for reassurance.

"I'll be here," promised Sia, her voice breaking as she felt choked with emotion.

Once Aarya left with Meera, Ritvik got up to sit close to Sia, taking her cold hands in his. "I'm sorry to spring Aarya on you like this Sia. I can see that it has been a shock. But please don't think I've been two-timing you. I'm a single father. Aarya was born through surrogacy. I don't even know who her mother is."

Sia made a keening sound which reminded him of a wounded animal. But why? What must be upsetting her now? Ritvik's breath caught in his throat. Did she also hate children like Dayanita did? It was Ritvik's turn to grow pale. But... but it hadn't seemed to be the case. Sia had held Aarya's hand from the moment she had woken up from her fainting spell. It wasn't the behaviour of someone who hated children. Feeling the pressure ease off his chest, Ritvik pulled Sia's head on to his shoulder as he hugged her. "What's wrong, honey?"

Sia shook her head. "You don't want to know."

"Why don't you try me?"

Sia pushed him away and got up, facing the other way. "I need to go."

Ritvik gave her an uncomprehending look. This was the same woman who couldn't have enough of him last night. What must have happened to change that?

Sia stood at the window which faced the same garden where she had met little Aarya. Her eyes shut in pain as she held the secret close to her heart, a secret which she was honour bound never to share with another living soul. But she had promised to wait for the child to return after her bath and Sia always kept her promises, at least she tried her best.

She turned when she heard the patter of little feet as Aarya rushed into the room, wearing a fresh pair of shorts and a t-shirt. "Sia Aunthie."

Sia went down on her haunches to hug the little girl close to her heart, her nose buried into the freshly powdered neck, her eyes shut tightly. No, she would *not* cry.

Ritvik watched helplessly as the woman he had fallen in love with bonded with his daughter, even as she refused to meet his gaze.

Where was the hitch?!

Sia left in fifteen minutes, refusing to stay despite repeated requests from both Ritvik and his daughter. Neither of them knew how it killed her to walk out of his home that evening.

18

Sia went to Cleopatra's to pick her handbag, not saying much to the others before leaving. She went home and dumped her bag along with her cell phone before leaving again immediately. She needed to be alone and knew for a fact that Ritvik would try to get in touch. And he was the one person she did not want to talk to right now.

Hugging her arms around her body, she walked over the bridge which connected the manmade island on which the hotel stood, to cross over to the mainland, to be lost among the crowds. And crowded it was. Sia kept walking, not really taking anything in, her jaw clenched even as silent tears continued to pour down her cheeks.

Sia had been a couple of months over seventeen when Badal and his father Kanhaiya had come calling at her home. From a lower middle-class family, Sia had somehow managed to complete her schooling, while her younger brother Shyam was in Std VI. Like any typical young woman from a small town, Sia had been brought up with getting married as the ultimate goal in life.

Her mother Ahalya rushed into the kitchen once she got to know the reason for their guests' visit to their home. "Sia, these people have come to ask for your hand in marriage." Her voice wobbled with emotion when she gave her daughter the news. "Heat water for some tea... no, wait, you go and get dressed up. I'll make the tea." Sia's mother was totally nervous.

Sia looked up at her mother with her eyes gone wide, her long, curly hair in a single braid, her eyes thickly lined with kohl. "Are you serious, Mamma?"

"Yes, I am." Ahalya nodded her head vigorously. "Your Pappa is talking to them right now. He has even invited Damodhar*ji* over." Damodhar doubled as both the astrologer and the *panditji* for the family.

Sia gulped. "Er... did you...?" She was short of words, too shy to ask her mother how the prospective groom appeared.

"I saw the boy." Ahalya smiled, calming down as she looked at her beautiful daughter. "His name is Badal and he is twenty-three years old. It is just his father and him at home. Poor boy! His mother died when he was barely fifteen. And no, his father never married again."

"Er..." Her mother had still not answered her unspoken question.

"Badal is handsome." Ahalya patted Sia's reddening cheek. "I'm sure he'll make a perfect husband for you. You know, he has studied up to Std VIII."

"Mamma, but..." Sia was confused.

"You know that it really doesn't matter Sia. He has a good job in a factory and is earning a monthly salary of six thousand rupees. He'll keep you like a queen. But then, let us wait for Damodharji and find out what he has to say about the match. You go on and get ready," instructed Ahalya as she placed a steel vessel with water on the gas stove, adding crushed ginger and sugar to it. "Wear that yellow *churidhar-kameez*. You appear best in that one."

"Okay, Mamma." Sia slipped out from the back door of the kitchen and went into the small room she shared with her brother, without entering the hall where the guests were sitting with her father Eknath. She wiped her face with a damp towel before applying some powder from her compact, checking to see that the kohl she had applied in the morning hadn't run over. She quickly changed into the clothes her mother had suggested before removing a gold chain with a pendant along with a matching pair of earrings from her cupboard and wearing them. She was ready to meet Badal after applying some cheap perfume which she hid among her clothes, out of her brother's reach.

Restless, Sia went back to the kitchen by the same way she had come and was startled to see that her mother wasn't there. Ahalya had joined the guests in the hall and it was obvious that Damodharji had also arrived as she heard three male voices chatting amicably, laughing loudly from time to time. The third voice must belong to Badal's father. She was curious to hear Badal's voice, but maybe he was too shy to speak.

What should she do now? Ahalya had obviously served them tea. Should she just wait here to be called or would it be alright if she walked out there? Sia recalled what her school friend Falak had told her about her own experience six months back, when her groom-to-be had come visiting for the first time. Her mother had made her wait and wait for two whole hours before she had got to meet the man who had later become her husband.

Sia sighed. She would have to wait, she supposed. Her mother would come and call her. On edge and fidgety, she stirred the *dal* simmering in a pot which was placed over a low flame on the stove.

"Sia, come *beta*." Ahalya came to fetch her.

Her heart in her throat, Sia walked behind her mother, her step hesitant. She had been raring to meet the man until a few seconds ago. But now, she wanted to just run the other way. Clenching her hands, Sia stepped into the hall, her eyes heavy with shyness.

"Sia, *meri beti*." Eknath called to her cheerfully as he put out his hand encouragingly. "Come here. Touch Kanhaiya*ji*'s feet and take his blessings."

Sia looked in the direction of Badal's father who was probably in his forties, with a head full of thick hair which was still black and an even thicker moustache. He smiled at her, showing all of his yellowed teeth. Curbing a shudder, she bent down to touch the man's feet.

"God bless you, my child. Badal is truly lucky. This is my son."

Sia gave the younger man a lightning look, before lowering her gaze. But that split second was enough to thrill her. Badal was fair and good looking with big, dark eyes and a sharp nose. He was many inches taller than her. Her heart beating loudly, Sia thought they would make a lovely pair if they got married.

"Sit down, Sia." Ahalya held her daughter by the hand and sat her down on a chair, in Badal's line of vision.

After that, Sia stole many surreptitious glances at Badal and liked him more and more each time she eyed him.

The surprise came when the father-son duo offered ten thousand rupees to Sia's family to take her home as Badal's bride.

Ahalya protested to her husband once their guests had gone. "How can we take money? It is we who have to give them dowry."

"Don't be stupid Ahalya. Goddess Mahalaxmi has come searching for us. Sia is a lucky child. I have spoken to Damodhar*ji*. He has checked both their horoscopes and insists that it's a match made in heaven." Eknath was a miser and couldn't believe his luck that he had got such an alliance walk into their home, offering for his daughter's hand.

Ahalya remained unconvinced, but her husband refused to listen to her.

Sia floated in a dream world as arrangements took place quickly and the day of her marriage arrived in barely three weeks. Badal and Sia made a beautiful couple when they took the *saat phere* around the ceremonial fire even as Damodhar*ji* chanted mantras, before they tied the knot.

Badal was gentle with his wife on their wedding night, making Sia a joyful bride. "I'm sure we will have a happy life together," he told her after quickly helping her undress. While feeling shy, Sia was also fascinated with the physical side of marriage. Falak had spoken about what all her husband had done to her on her wedding night. At the end of it, Sia decided that Badal was even better as she went to sleep, her head against her new husband's shoulder and a smile on her face.

Five months went by with Sia running their small home efficiently, managing the cooking and cleaning as she served both, her husband and father-in-law.

That evening, Badal came home a couple of hours earlier than usual. "Sia, I need to go on an official tour to Jaipur for five days. Pack my clothes for me and *haan*, also some *rotis* and *sabzi* for my meal on the train."

"What?" Sia rushed after him into their bedroom. "Why suddenly?" Hugging him from behind, she said, "I will miss you terribly."

Badal laughed. "It will be only for five days, Sia. I will be back before you miss me."

"Five days! You are talking as if it's only five hours."

"*Pagli*." He kissed her on her cheek, before patting it. "I need to leave in an hour. You had better get everything together fast."

Sia pouted at him before packing his stuff swiftly and efficiently. She went to the kitchen and cooked a fresh meal and packed it in a stainless-steel tiffin box. "Here you go, all ready."

"Good girl." Badal turned to his father who was sitting on a chair watching TV. "I will be off, Pappa. You take care. I will return on Wednesday." With a wave to both of them, he walked out of the door.

Sia felt a bit sad as she missed her husband already. She also wished she had known that he wasn't going to be there. She could have at least visited her parents during that time. But then, they were so far away from Jhunjhunu, where she lived with her husband and father-in-law, about sixteen hours by train. She couldn't visit them whenever she pleased. It needed a lot of planning and budgeting. And then there was Kanhaiya, Badal's father. Being the only woman in the house, it was Sia's responsibility to prepare his meals. With a deep sigh, Sia lay back on her bed, her arm across her eyes.

She woke up with a start when she heard the door to her bedroom shut. Sia couldn't believe her eyes when she saw Kanhaiya standing in front of her, wearing only the leery grin which showed his yellowed teeth and not much else.

It was almost four years after her marriage to Badal when Sia sat in front of Ruhi Chaddha, her therapist. It was their fifth session and finally Sia was opening up, slowly but steadily. "I felt betrayed when the man I had married, the one who had promised to protect me, thought it was absolutely normal for his father to have his way with me." Sia paused, her voice choking as she recalled her marriage which had remained blissful for all of only five months. Her life had become one long nightmare after that. She shuddered when she recalled that night when the man who she had treated like a father, had molested her.

Once she had begun, the words tumbled over each other to get out, as Sia let the poison out of her system, one drop at a time. She had hated both the father and the son. But was there a way out of this hell?

"I became pregnant after a few months." Tears poured down Sia's face as she confessed to Ruhi during the eighth sitting. Her voice lowered to a horrified whisper as she continued, "I didn't even know whose child was growing in my belly. That's when I decided I can't let the baby be born. Imagine the shame of the child! It was enough I was living in that gutter. Why bring another being into it? I aborted the baby. It was a good thing I fell sick for many months after that, keeping both men away from me." Her voice was dry now, without emotion.

"What about your parents? Couldn't you have spoken to them?"

Sia's gaze met the therapist's for a few moments before she bent down to look at her feet. "I could maybe have talked to my mother. But she had a heart condition and I didn't want to make it worse." How many times had she toyed with the idea of telling her mother? But the times they spoke to each other—

maybe once in a month—it had all been about Ahalya's deteriorating health. Her mother had passed on two years ago due to heart disease. There were no tears left in Sia by now.

"Do you have friends?"

Falak! Yes, she had been her friend from Junior KG. Sia nodded. "Yes, her name is Falak."

"Did you try talking to her?"

Sia shook her head, saying nothing. What was the use? Falak had a beautiful—secure, actually—life with her husband and son. How could Sia have told her about her own dreadful life? She had considered it. But every time she tried, Sia had been struck with a new worry. What if Falak became so ashamed of her childhood friend that she stopped talking to Sia after knowing this? What if Falak thought there was something wrong with Sia and that's why her life was so terrible? Worse yet, what if Falak laughed at her? Or even called her a liar? What if...?

"Why not go to the police?"

Sia gave Ruhi a strange look, a frown on her face. "Police? But people go to them when there's a theft or a murder, right? How could I have gone to the police for this?"

Ruhi Chaddha looked at the girl in front of her, her gaze sympathetic. "So, what did you do?"

"Nothing until that day when Kanhaiya brought his friend home and Badal wanted me to service that man. That's when..."

Sia didn't know what had come over her that day. She had quietly gone to the back of their house to pick up a long and thick stick from the pile of firewood which was stored there for heating water in a big copper boiler. She had walked into the bedroom to thrash the man. She had gone berserk as she beat him up to an inch of his life.

It was only when Badal and Kanhaiya had returned home after a few drinks at the local tavern when they discovered the unconscious man. Struck by fear, the duo had taken the man to a local clinic.

"The police came then, asking questions. I realised that I had nothing to lose by then. There was no one who cared anyway. I told them everything. Then the senior inspector brought this lady from the NGO and Kamini madam took me to her house."

The wife of a millionaire with no children of her own, Kamini ran an NGO for the homeless. She kept going to the local police station to rescue people. On that particular day, it was sheer luck that she had contacted the police inspector and met Sia. Despite having dealt with the terrible circumstances of those she helped, she was shaken by Sia's story. It was Kamini who had decided that Sia needed therapy.

Kamini had also got her lawyer to file for divorce and sued Badal for a one-time alimony settlement of two lakh rupees. She had advised Sia to also file a case against the father and son for rape. But Sia didn't want to have anything else to do with them. "I don't want to see their faces ever again, madam. If you can get me some work, it will be a great help."

"Let me see if I can find a way to get you trained for something—tailoring, beautician or something else."

For the first time in six months, Kamini saw a spark of interest appear in Sia's grey gaze. "Beautician training, is that possible?"

Kamini smiled. "Yes."

Sia trained as a beautician locally at Jhunjhunu. She also went to English conversation classes. With Kamini's constant support and encouragement, coupled with the therapy sessions, Sia gained her lost confidence, slowly but steadily. Yes, she still took time to get friendly with people and her smile was hesitant most of the time unlike her usual self. But Sia worked on it, day and night, and slowly regained even the sense of humour which she had lost. Being among people of her own age at the classes helped her heal a lot. And there was no need for shame as they didn't know anything about her life with Badal and Kanhaiya.

Once the three-month beautician course was over, Sia asked Kamini something which truly impressed the latter. "Madam, is it possible for me to learn karate? Someone at the English classes said that it's good for defending oneself against an attacker. What do you think?"

"I think it's a great idea Sia. You should learn the art. But the course is prolonged. Are you ready for it?"

Sia decided to give it a try and managed to reach the level of a blue belt. She felt it was enough to keep her safe.

And then, a couple of months later, when Sia was feeling as good as normal, she decided it was time to move on. She didn't want to live in the same town as her ex. Taking Kamini's advice, she moved to Delhi and got a job at a salon. She worked hard at three different beauty parlours over the next few months, but the money which came in was zilch.

Then, one day, she came across an ad for the London Beauty School. With fire in her belly, Sia decided that that was where she wanted to train. It required a lot of money though. Working in small parlours, she wouldn't be able to earn that kind of money over the next fifty years.

Sia called Kamini, the only person who had shown her compassion. "Madam, I am interested in doing this course in London. It's expensive…"

"Let me know how much. I'll sponsor you." Kamini was all encouragement.

Sia shook her head. The woman had already done so much for her. Realising that Kamini couldn't see her, she said, "Madam, I don't think it's fair to make you pay for this. I just want you to guide me about how I can get that kind of money. It's okay even if it's a loan. I will pay it all back when I get a good job later."

Kamini didn't respond for a few seconds. "I'll call you tomorrow, Sia. By then, I hope I have an answer for you."

With hope fluttering in her heart, Sia cut the call.

The next day, instead of phoning her, Kamini went to Delhi to meet Sia personally. "Sit down, Sia." Kamini patted the stool next to hers. "I have an opportunity for you. Have you heard of surrogacy or hiring a womb?"

Sia stared blankly at the other woman. "I don't understand."

"There is a rich man who doesn't have a wife. But he wants a child. He is ready to pay a lot of money to the woman who will bear his child. I..."

"Will I have to live with him?" Sia shuddered. She would not be forced to sleep with a stranger, for whatever reason.

Kamini shook her head, a hand on Sia's shoulder, her gaze gentle. "No *beta*. You don't even have to meet the man, nor do you need to know his name. It's the same with him. He will never know who his child's mother will be. If you are agreeable, we need to find out if you pass all the medical tests. I am not too worried in that regard since you underwent a batch of tests when the police gave you into my care. They need a woman who's in an excellent state of physical and mental health. I can stand guarantee for both in your case. And of course, your womb needs to be strong too. Usually, they insist that the woman should have given birth to at least one child. But well, there's nothing wrong with you getting impregnated since it has happened to you before, even if you didn't carry your baby full term."

"But how will I get pregnant?" Sia was confused. Though she trusted Kamini totally.

"It's done in a doctor's clinic, artificially. If you are willing, I will set the ball rolling. This man has already tried with other women and it has not been successful. He is ready to pay ten lakh rupees for it. They will take care of your stay, your food and your medical expenses, not just during pregnancy, but three months after that, until you recover completely. One thing though, the baby will never be yours. You cannot meet the child, ever, once it's taken away, which will be within a few hours of the baby's birth."

Sia looked at Kamini with wide eyes. Was what the lady saying even possible? Why couldn't the man get married? And how will he bring the child up without a mother? And closer to home, can she give away her child, just like that? Sia asked Kamini if she could take some time to think about it.

Ten lakh rupees was a lot of money. It would cover her travel and training expenses, while also allowing her to have some decent savings, if she managed the money properly.

Actually, what was there to think? Did Sia really have a choice? And where was the harm? She just had to give her 'womb on hire' as Kamini madam called it. She will be careful not to get attached to the baby. She won't even get to spend a few hours with it after it was born. She only needed to spend the forty weeks with the baby in her uterus. Sia knew she would manage. If she really thought about it, the arrangement seemed too simple and easy. She called Kamini the next day to tell her that she would do it.

Sia quit her job to go to Udaipur, as directed by Kamini, and admitted herself into a private nursing home. They conducted a battery of medical tests on her over one whole week, asking her a million questions. Kamini had given her clear instructions not to talk too much about her traumatic life.

Once she was pronounced fit, the process of getting her pregnant via artificial insemination began. Sia didn't understand most of what they said. Her only confidence was in Kamini madam. And then there was the fact that an advance of three lakh rupees had been deposited in a bank account which was opened for her.

Sia became pregnant in the first attempt, much to the joy of the team of doctors. She moved to a service apartment not very far from the clinic where fresh vegetables, fruits, eggs, meat and provisions were delivered to her, twice in a week. She also had a weekly appointment with the gynaecologist. Sia enjoyed exceptionally good health and followed the doctor's instructions to the T.

Nine months later, her baby daughter was born.

Sia stared at the newborn in her arms, unable to stop the powerful feeling of love which engulfed her. The little one was barely three hours old, sleeping soundly as Sia held her close to her heart. No, she must not cry, Sia kept telling herself. Wasn't the birth of a baby a celebration? How could she shed tears on the event then? She knew what she had signed up for, a year ago. Her womb had been hired by some rich man to give life to his baby and disappear from its life the moment her job was done. She had signed the contract with her eyes wide open, for after all, she needed the money.

Why the hell had nobody warned her that she might get attached to the infant which had been separated from her the moment the doctor cut the umbilical cord?

Sia wanted to protest when a nurse walked in to take the baby from her. No! That was her blood, her flesh, her genes, her firstborn that they were taking away from her. She didn't want to let go of her baby daughter. All those words rushed through her mind, but remained unspoken, as she watched in silence as her daughter was whisked away, never to be seen again.

Sia came back to the present, wiping her eyes as she walked up the stairs to her apartment and wasn't really surprised when she found Ritvik waiting for her outside the door.

19

Ritvik looked at Sia's red eyes and swollen face and wanted to hold her in his arms until her pain went away. But she moved away when he lifted a hand to touch her face. Not keen to force himself into her space, he let his hand drop; though he made it clear with his body language that he wasn't going anywhere until he got to the bottom of her misery.

Sia opened the door to her flat and walked in, exhausted. She turned around to stop Ritvik from entering, or at least tried to. "Can't it wait until tomorrow, whatever you want to say? I am too tired."

"No."

"Eh?!" She looked up at him, her arms crossed over the front of her body. Had she heard him right?

"I said no. It can't wait till tomorrow. Have you had something to eat?"

The thought of food made Sia want to throw up. "I'm not hungry."

He smiled at her, though it was a caricature, very unlike his usual broad one. "Will it make a difference if I say that I'm hungry and want to eat?"

Sia hesitated only for a second before shaking her head firmly. "No, it wouldn't." She needed to be firm with him or Ritvik might simply sweep her off her feet all over again. He had seemed like a demigod—and she didn't mean only his looks—after Badal and his father. But... but, how could she be in a relationship with Ritvik, now that she knew what she did?

"You're being cruel." Ritvik looked at her, hoping to revive her sense of humour. But it didn't work.

"I suppose I am. Is there a purpose to this conversation, Ritvik?"

"Sarcasm doesn't sit well on you."

Sia sighed. "Do tell me what you came to say. I have an early morning appointment tomorrow."

Ritvik leaned against the door, wondering what must have gone wrong. In fact, that's what he had been thinking about for hours. It had begun from the time Sia met Aarya. He was sure it had something to do with his daughter. "Listen, Sia. I know you're upset that I didn't tell you about Aarya. It's not that I wanted to keep my daughter a secret from you." He sighed deeply before continuing. "I was so excited when she was born that I couldn't talk of anything else. Over the next six months or so, every dialogue was peppered with 'Aarya this' and 'Aarya that'. It didn't strike me that it was only me enjoying the conversation as it was my daughter I was talking about. The others were bored but were too polite to say anything, until one day, Akhil explained to me how I was going overboard with my enthusiasm of becoming a father. Maybe it would have been different if I had Aarya's mother to share it with. I don't know," he shrugged. "From then on, I consciously stopped talking about Aarya to anyone, unless someone actually came up and asked me about her. Since we got closer, I was keen that you and Aarya should meet. Only I never expected it to come as such a shock to you."

Sia stood there quietly, listening to Ritvik. Why the hell did he have to make her fall in love with him more and more? He truly had a golden heart. She turned away without replying as tears welled in her eyes. Her surrogacy contract had clearly stated that she should never try to contact her child or its father. And she should never talk about it if she ever came to know who they were. How could she break the contract? Hadn't she taken the money for it? Sia felt torn.

She turned a startled face towards Ritvik when she felt his warm hands on her shoulders. "Sia... I'm in love with you." Ritvik spoke softly in her ear. "I never, ever expected to say this to any woman, not in this life."

Sia was moved to hear his words despite herself as she turned and buried her face in his chest, her whole body trembling as if in a fever.

Ritvik's large hand stroked down her back gently, having the calming effect which his words couldn't achieve. "I dated a few women in my time and had some affairs too. I hope I don't sound arrogant, but I felt that they couldn't see beyond my looks and my bank balance. I have a wonderful mother and an equally awesome sister. That should have told me that all women couldn't be bad. But I suppose you can call me hot headed when one fine day, immediately after my last affair, I decided I never wanted a wife."

To be truthful, Ritvik couldn't recall the woman's name or face, the one who had called him names, insisting that he was like a male prostitute, free with his sculpted body, leading innocent women down the depraving path of craving, before leaving them high and dry. She had known what she was getting into when they started the affair. Only she had changed her mind and demanded to marry Ritvik when she realised how rich he actually was. Her words had hurt his ego badly enough for him to decide to stay away from women, forever. Or so he had thought!

"But I loved the thought of having a baby of my own. Having read about surrogate children sired by the likes of Aamir Khan and Shah Rukh Khan, I thought, why not for myself? I didn't speak about it to my family. I knew they would have never agreed. I informed them only after Aarya was born. Tell you what, Sia? That's one decision I'll never regret. I adored Aarya from the second my eyes fell on her. Now, three years after I took that drastic decision of not marrying ever, I'm facing a change of mind. Sia..." He lifted her chin to look down at her. "Will you marry me?"

Ritvik had expected anything but for Sia to bawl her heart out as she left his arms to go sit on a sofa, her bent knees tucked under her chin and her arms around her legs as she rocked herself. Looking at her, one would think that her world was at an end.

Ritvik went on his knees on the floor beside her, his hand on her shoulder. "Sia, what's wrong? How can I help you if you don't tell me?"

Sia shook her head. "No one can help me."

"Honey, listen to me. I..."

"Please go."

Sia felt both relief and anguish when Ritvik got up immediately. What would she do if he walked out of her life right now?

But being who he was, Ritvik lifted her from the sofa before sitting down again to hold her in his lap. "I'm going nowhere. You don't talk about it if you don't want to, but you're stuck with me. I know you love me too. And I don't think anything else matters."

Sia's sobs reduced to hiccups as she sat there with Ritvik's arms locked around her securely. What was she to do now?

She raised her face to look up at him. Maybe, just maybe, he would run away if he saw how horrendous she looked with her face all swollen and her nose red. Her nerves cracking under pressure, a giggle escaped Sia.

"Glad to know that you find something funny. Wanna share the joke with me?" Ritvik brushed the curls away from her forehead as he would have done to Aarya. A curious look passed over his face as he eyed her cork screw curls which were so like his daughter's. He smiled at Sia, an eyebrow raised, waiting for her answer.

"I don't think you can still be in love with me, not after seeing my face as it is now." Sia looked at Ritvik pathetically, pressing a hand against her chest as she felt her heart breaking.

Without uttering a word, Ritvik kissed her forehead, before pressing his lips to a swollen eyelid which felt hot to the touch. His mouth moved to her cheek, then her nose, before he claimed her lips in a deep kiss. The kiss wasn't one of passion, it wasn't one of lust. It was a kiss which connected deeply with her heart, reassuring Sia that he was hers, in sickness and health, forever. He took her hand and placed it against his heart which beat steadily. He lifted his head to look at her. "Tell me something, Sia. Will you run away if I break my nose or maybe lose my teeth or whatever? Will you hate me if I lose my looks?"

"Don't be an idiot, Ritvik. Do you think I love you only for your appearance?" Sia wrinkled her nose in distaste.

"Exactly." Ritvik laughed softly as he buried his face against her neck.

Sia sighed, realising that she couldn't win this argument. It was another story that she didn't want to. Her hand brushed over the back of his head of its own volition. "Ritvik, have you ever felt curious about Aarya's mother?"

Ritvik straightened to look at Sia. "A lot of times. But then, she must have moved on. Even if I meet her today, she is not the one I would want to marry. Aarya's life, in fact, all our lives would be less complicated if I didn't meet the woman. For all I know, she has her own family and wouldn't want me or Aarya to intrude."

"What if I told you that Aarya's mother hasn't moved on and pines for her?" Sia was pale as she asked him the question. She had suddenly decided that it was best to bring things out into the open and see where it took her. To hell with the contract! She didn't think Ritvik would actually sue her. The worst he would do was to chuck her out of his life and her job. Well, it was time to find out.

"How would you know?" Ritvik looked deeply into Sia's smoky grey eyes, his heart beat going up by several notches. "Have you met her? How do you know she's Aarya's mother? Where does she live?"

"Wait!" Sia got up and went to her cupboard and rummaged within for a few minutes before going to sit on the sofa next to his. "See this."

Ritvik took the grainy, coloured photograph which she offered. It was of a couple with a little girl between them who was holding their hands. His eyes went wide with shock. The child could have been Aarya except that the photo was pretty old. He turned to look at Sia, stupefaction in his charcoal gaze. "Who's this?"

Sia looked at him steadily. "The couple are my parents."

The photo fell out of Ritvik's hand as he jumped up from his chair, an expression of wonderment on his handsome face. "You are Aarya's mother."

20

It took Sia more than an hour to persuade Ritvik to leave. He had been excited, instead of upset, when he found out that Sia was his daughter's mother and had been confident she would marry him now. He got someone to bring dinner for the two of them from Emperor Akbar, chatting with her cheerfully as they ate the food.

Ritvik gave Sia his trademark grin, his face completely devoid of tension as he held her hand. "No wonder you fainted when you saw Aarya. It must have been such a shock. I know it's going to take some time, but I don't think it'll be too difficult for you and Aarya to get to know each other. I'm so glad that I won't need to lie to her when I introduce you as her mother as well as her Daddy's wife, if you know what I mean."

Sia gave him a brief nod, dazed at the pace at which he was making plans. He didn't know a damn thing about her earlier life. Ritvik might not run away from a swollen face, but he would definitely not want to have anything to do with her once he knew the kind of life she had led a few years ago. But now was not the time to enlighten him. More than anything, Sia didn't want to push Ritvik into a corner. He shouldn't feel forced to marry her out of pity. And she knew for a fact that no self-respecting man would want to wed her once he knew the truth about her past life.

Sia pretended to eat, chewing long and hard as she swallowed small bites of food, drinking a lot of water in between to keep it down. It was obvious that Ritvik had no plans to leave any time soon.

Ritvik knew she was tired and beat. It wasn't as if he wanted to make love to her. But he wanted to hold Sia in his arms and soothe away all the hurt and pain she had suffered, not just in the last few hours, but from the time she gave birth to their baby and gave her away selflessly.

But Sia was firm. "Please Ritvik, go home. I need some time to myself."

"Are you sure?" He looked deeply into her eyes which were so like his daughter's, now that he was aware enough to notice the resemblance. "You won't cry, will you?"

Sia gave him a small smile which didn't quite reach her eyes. "Why would I do that?"

"Yeah, actually, why would you do that?" Ritvik gathered her in his arms and held her close to his heart, rubbing his chin on the top of her head. "Sleep in late. Boss's orders."

"Haha! Let me think about it." She had to literally push him out of her apartment, her heart heavy.

Sia went to bed, though sleep refused to come. She had a wonderful job. She adored the man who loved her with all of his heart. She could finally reconnect with the baby which she had given up for good. Shouldn't she be on top of the world?

But then, how could Sia drag Ritvik down to the gutter from where she had come? Sia felt too exhausted to run away from the situation. Could she persuade Ritvik to give up the idea of marriage? Sleep took over finally once Sia convinced herself that she could.

Sia had a busy morning and messaged Ritvik telling him so. Otherwise, she knew that he would want to meet her as soon as possible. She needed to still think of a way to dissuade him from the idea of marrying her.

She stepped out into the compound to take a walk after lunch, unable to stop the smile on her face when she read Ritvik's reply. "Don't think you can escape me forever." The words were followed by a red heart. Sia knew that he loved her. Otherwise, those very same words would have made her quake in terror.

Sia raised her head when she heard a car engine running even as it was standing under a huge banyan tree. She didn't know what made her stop behind the tree when she heard Aarya's childish prattle. "Where we goin'?"

"Daddy is waiting for you. He asked me to bring you." A large man, dressed all in black, held the child's—her child's—hand as they walked to the nondescript car.

Sia had seen the man before, though she didn't know his name. He worked for Maharaja International.

But where was he taking Aarya? Her maternal instincts kicked in, her mind playing havoc as she remembered the horrors a girl could face, even if she was as little as Aarya. She quickly clicked a picture of the car's license plate as she went closer, half bent, hoping against hope not to be noticed. She twisted the lock on the trunk to find it open. She lifted it a little before jumping in, just as the car took off.

It was only two minutes later when Sia wondered why the hell she hadn't screamed for help. She quickly messaged Ritvik. "Where are you?" She put her phone on 'vibrate' mode.

It was at least twenty minutes before she saw the two blue ticks appear next to her message.

"In a meeting in my office," came the reply.

Her instincts had been right.

She sent him a picture of the license plate. "Someone picked Aarya up in this car. I managed to get into the trunk. We've been travelling for twenty minutes."

"What the fuck!" Ritvik swore when he saw Sia's latest message and called her immediately, only to have her cut his call.

He slapped a hand on his desk, getting up from his chair, anxiety and fury churning his stomach.

Sia was relieved to see two more blue ticks appear against her latest message. Which meant that Ritvik had seen the message even if he hadn't replied.

"What's wrong?" Indrajeet Thakore got up too when he noticed Ritvik's agitation.

Ritvik looked at the other man with a frown as if wondering what he was doing in his office. They had been discussing about the paying guest accommodation which Indrajeet was planning to start in one section of his family property.

"Just give me a minute, Jeet. There's some kind of an emergency." Ritvik walked out of his office, calling Meghnath on his cell.

Sia could hear a phone ringing in the car. She strained her ears to hear what the man was saying.

"Meghnath, where are you? There's an emergency. I need..."

"Sir, I'm out. It's my day off."

"But this is urgent. Can you come now?"

"I'm sorry sir. But I am not in town."

"Shit!" Ritvik disconnected the phone. Sia had said they were about twenty minutes away, twenty-five now. He turned around, only to knock against Indrajeet who had followed him out of the office.

"Jeet, shall we meet later? I'll give you a call. I..."

"What's up? I can help you maybe?"

Ritvik's brow cleared. Yes, maybe. "Just a minute. Let me send this message first." Ritvik messaged quickly to Sia, "Keep sending me your location on WhatsApp every five minutes or so."

"Okay." She followed his instruction.

Ritvik jumped into his low-slung BMW and gestured for Indrajeet to climb in.

"Here, look for WhatsApp updates from Sia and give me directions."

Indrajeet took Ritvik's phone and instructed him to turn left after crossing the bridge into the city.

"I don't know what the hell's happening. It looks like my daughter has been kidnapped." Ritvik spoke swiftly, with no emotion in his voice.

Indrajeet jerked, almost dropping the iPhone which he was holding, before he turned to stare at Ritvik, his jaw wide open in shock. He quickly scrolled through the messages above and immediately recognised the picture of the license plate. The car belonged to the Thakores. Had his grandmother gone mad? Hadn't he told her clearly not to do anything drastic like this?

21

In her anxiety to ensure that Ritvik was on track, Sia hadn't bothered to check if her phone had enough power. Her eyes went wide in shock when it flickered and went off. Oh my God! What should she do now? She didn't even know Ritvik's cell number by heart, just in case she got her hands on another phone. Before panic could set in, she felt the car engine switch off and heard a door open.

She calculated that it must be a little less than an hour since they left the hotel. She opened the boot a couple of inches to check out her surroundings. There was no noise of traffic. It was obviously somewhere secluded.

"Daddhie is here?"

Sia didn't think twice before jumping out. She didn't want Aarya to panic when she realised that her father wasn't around.

"Yes," answered the man, before they turned right from where the car was parked. Sia followed as quietly as possible. But the man turned around suddenly and saw Sia, a shocked expression on his face.

Sia took a few steps to reach them even as Aarya squealed delightedly. "Sia Aunthie."

"Aarya darling." Sia put out her arms to her daughter, who jumped into them in joy.

"Uncle broughth me to see Daddhie."

Meghnath was dazed. He had recognised Sia Rathod as Cleopatra's manager the moment he saw her. What the hell was she doing here? It looked like Ritvik's daughter also knew the woman. In a way it was a good thing. Otherwise, the child might have started howling her heart out when she found out that her father was nowhere in the vicinity.

But then, the game had turned dangerous now with Sia Rathod recognising him. What the hell! He had better call Rajmata Santhini Devi at the first opportunity.

"Why have you brought Aarya here?" Sia deliberately kept her voice soft, not wanting to panic the little girl. But her gaze was sharp as she looked boldly into the huge man's eyes. He was even taller than Ritvik.

"Er... ma'am, sir asked me to bring her here."

"To this broken down *haveli*?" Sia asked with a frown, looking at the dilapidated structure behind the man.

"Yes ma'am," Meghnath insisted, his voice stronger than before.

Sia bit her lip, wondering what to do. How would Ritvik find them with her phone switched off? She had given her location about fifteen minutes back or so. She decided to play it cool. She walked with Aarya and sat down on the porch step, holding the little one in her lap. "Are you okay, sweetie?"

"Hmm... sleepy." Aarya tucked her thumb into her mouth, placing her head on Sia's shoulder, going to sleep within seconds.

Sia felt such a deep gush of love spread through her as she held little Aarya in her arms. Forgetting all about their circumstances, she gathered the child closer to her chest, hugging her tight, even as tears threatened to engulf her. Somehow, she seemed to have lost control of her emotions since the bout of crying yesterday. But no, Sia refused to let them fall, her fingers crossed at Aarya's back as she willed and willed that Ritvik came looking for them. She was glad he was at least aware that Aarya was with her mother.

She looked around from the corner of her eyes to see the kidnapper—he must be one, for sure—talking on the phone. So far, it looked like it was only the three of them here. Thank God the man hadn't tried to lock or tie the two of them somewhere inside the broken-down structure.

In the meanwhile, Santhini Devi was shouting at Meghnath. "Why did you take the child without asking me first, Meghnath? I didn't want you to do it," she screamed.

Meghnath was totally confused. "But Rajmata, I joined the hotel as a bouncer just for this purpose, right? You had only told me to do so." He was built like a truck, but a softie from within. Taking a leaf out of his father's book, Meghnath worshipped the ground the old matriarch walked on and was ready to lay down his life for her. When she had told him that he should join Maharaja International as an employee, he had done just that and had been working for Ritvik Bansal over the last six months. It was only ten days ago when the Rajmata had revealed her plan to have the Bansal child kidnapped. He was to ensure the kid was neither scared nor intimidated. The Rajmata had promised to handle Ritvik Bansal once the child was hidden away from him. And that was exactly the reason why Meghnath had brought Aarya Bansal to the old *haveli* and called Santhini Devi immediately. How was he to know that the Rajmata had changed her mind overnight?

"You take the child right back to her father, this very minute," ordered Santhini Devi firmly. She was a mite disturbed at the turn of events. It was true that she had given Meghnath the instructions to kidnap the child. But that was before her grandson Indrajeet had made her promise not to do exactly that. It had completely blown out of her mind that Meghnath was going to do it today. What a situation!

"*Theek hai*, Rajmata. I'll take the child back immediately." Meghnath always followed Santhini Devi's instructions implicitly.

He turned around to walk towards Sia Rathod and Aarya, a soft look on his hard face when he noticed the child was fast asleep. "Ma'am, please come along, I am taking you back to the hotel."

"What?" Sia stared at the man as if he had taken leave of his senses. "Why bring Aarya here in the first place?"

Meghnath turned a funny shade of purple, to Sia's amazement. "I'm sorry, ma'am. It was a mistake."

"Do you realise that your mistake can land you in jail?"

Meghnath felt stupid as he looked into her blazing eyes. "I... I don't..." He paused as they both turned their heads when they heard the sound of a car engine.

Sia smiled even as Meghnath scowled when they saw Ritvik's BMW enter the compound.

Ritvik drove for thirty-five minutes, following Indrajeet's directions before the messages from Sia stopped coming. But by now, Indrajeet had guessed where the car must have headed. It was going in the direction of an old *haveli* which had been in the Thakore family for over four centuries. It was situated in a nearby village which was about fifty minutes from the Udaipur City Palace. He didn't tell Ritvik that Sia's phone had probably conked off as the updates had stopped, but continued to give him directions as he knew the way like the back of his own hand.

They arrived at the property twenty minutes later and Ritvik stopped his car right behind the one which was already parked there. He immediately recognised the number plate from the picture Sia had sent. With a sigh of relief, he jumped out of the car even as Indrajeet got out from the other side.

Both men were running by now, though Indrajeet was two steps ahead as he turned right. He seemed to know where he was going, thought Ritvik, running beside him. The sight which greeted Ritvik's eyes made him pause, a soft smile lighting up his face. Aarya was sleeping peacefully in her mother's arms. He rushed over to their side, throwing his arms around both of them, having eyes for no one else.

Meghnath was aghast to see Indrajeet Thakore and Ritvik Bansal. What was *Kunwar Sa* doing here? Another five minutes and he could have escaped their wrath. He tried to smile at the furious Thakore scion who glared at him, his eyes blazing with temper. "Who set you up to this?" Indrajeet snarled.

Ritvik turned to see what was happening when he heard voices raised in argument. That's when he noticed Indrajeet shouting at... at the bouncer who worked for him. "What the hell are you doing here, Meghnath? I thought you told me you were on leave and not even in town when I called you some time back?" asked Ritvik, confusion on his face.

"I... I..." Meghnath refused to meet Ritvik's eyes, his huge frame slouched.

"I think I can answer your question."

Ritvik turned to Indrajeet when the latter spoke, surprise on his face. "What?"

Indrajeet shook his head, looking terribly upset. "It's my stupid grandmother with her idiotic schemes. I'm extremely sorry that you had to undergo such anxiety Ritvik. I..."

"I don't understand," said Ritvik, "Meghnath works for me, at Maharaja International." A deep frown gathered on his forehead as he looked from one man to the other.

"Meghnath is first and foremost my Grandmother Santhini Devi's bodyguard and Man Friday. His father used to work for us before him."

"If that was the case, then why did he take a job at my hotel? Wait! Let me see," Ritvik turned to address Meghnath, "Was it for the purpose of kidnapping my daughter?"

Meghnath looked at Ritvik and was shaken by the fury in the other man's black gaze. "I... I was simply following instructions," he said lamely.

"Jeet?" Ritvik turned to look at Indrajeet who appeared as enraged as he felt.

Giving a deep sigh, Indrajeet said, "Let me speak to my senile old grandmother."

"But Meghnath, how dare you?" Ritvik turned on the bouncer, his black eyes piercing. "I trusted you with my own life, expecting you to safeguard me and my hotel. This is betrayal of the worst kind." He would hate to go to the police, but then he couldn't let the man go scot free, could he?

Indrajeet laid a hand on Ritvik's arm. "Do you trust me to deal with him? I promise you that you won't have any trouble from my family from here on."

Ritvik stared searchingly into Indrajeet's eyes and saw only honesty there, the same that he had noticed in his father Gajendar's face. He nodded slowly. "I won't do anything this time, for your sake and your father's, Jeet. Just ensure that neither your grandmother nor Meghnath here step anywhere near me or my property, okay?"

Indrajeet nodded. "Absolutely."

"I'll see you tomorrow and we can continue the discussion which was interrupted." Ritvik shook Indrajeet's hand. Turning, he placed an arm around Sia's shoulder to guide her to his car. "Do you want me to take Aarya? She's probably too heavy for you."

Sia shook her head. "Not really. I'd like to hold her, if you don't mind."

"And why would I do that, honey?" Ritvik stopped to give her a kiss on her cheek. "I'm so glad you were around when that idiot decided to take off with Aarya. For a while, I was shaken that the hotel wasn't a secure place and Aarya didn't know she shouldn't go away with strangers. But," he sighed, "Meghnath was part of my security team *and* he was no stranger to Aarya." He picked his phone to see who it was when it rang. It was Meera Aunty.

"Ritvik, is Aarya with you? Meghnath had come to pick her. I just wanted to check."

Ritvik grinned, the relief obvious on his face. "Yes, Meera Aunty. Aarya's with me. But next time, please verify with me before sending her away with anyone. That idiot made a mistake and I had to chase him all around town before I reached Aarya." He didn't mention the actual situation. Why worry the old lady?

He disconnected the phone before talking to Sia. "That Santhini Devi is going to get it from me one of these days. Indrajeet Thakore," he nodded his head towards the other man who was getting into the car with Meghnath, "is as decent as they come. He's Dayanita's brother, by the way. Their father is also a gem of a man. But his grandmother is devil incarnate. Dayanita's probably taken after the woman. I..."

"Don't tell me it was the grandmother's idea to have Aarya..." Sia stopped mid-sentence when she felt her daughter stir awake in her arms.

"Daddhie, you came." Aarya grinned as she spread her arms wide to reach out to her father who was about to wear his seat belt.

"Sweetie." Ritvik enfolded his daughter in his arms, kissing her on her cheek. The past hour had been like hell on earth. It was lucky that he hadn't had time to think and only act, all thanks to Sia who had managed to save the day.

"Sia Aunthie also came. Aarya hungry. Pizza?" Aarya tilted her head to ask her father.

"Anything for you, imp. Let's go have pizza."

"Yaaayyy. Sia Aunthie come?"

"Yes, Sia too. Do you want to sit with her while I drive?"

Aarya nodded vigorously, moving into Sia's lap and hugging her tight.

Ritvik and Sia looked at each other, relief the predominant emotion in both their eyes. It was not just that Aarya was safe, it was also because the little girl had no idea of what all could have happened, safe from any trauma to carry forward or maim her for life.

Ritvik was glad that they were together as a family now. It won't be long before he and Sia got married. They could both tell Aarya that she also had a mummy now, same as little Mehul. Excited about the prospect, he kept dropping not too subtle hints throughout dinner, totally unaware that Sia couldn't take the pressure, not after yesterday's trauma and today's drama.

Extremely busy the next day, Ritvik had sent a message to Sia first thing in the morning and informed her that he would pick her up for dinner at eight. It was past seven in the evening when he reached into his in-tray to check for papers left there for his attention. His eyes immediately fell on the lavender envelope with just his first name on it in an unknown handwriting.

With a sense of foreboding, he pulled out the single sheet of paper and looked at the signature and wasn't really surprised when he saw "Sia" scrolled there.

His face grim, Ritvik read the brief note:

My Dear Ritvik,

Thank you so much for bringing up our daughter so beautifully. I couldn't have asked for a better father for my baby girl. For reasons which are beyond my control, I cannot ever be your wife. I thank my lucky stars to have known you and been your lover, even if it was for only a brief period. It was the best time of my life. I wish you and little Aarya a wonderful life.

Goodbye,
Sia

What the fuck!!!!!!!!

22

anthini Devi stared at her eldest grandson, never having seen this facet of him before now. The boy she knew was generally calm, collected and respectful of all his elders. Even the other day, he had been angry, but nothing like today. Just now, Indrajeet was in a flaming temper, all set to bring the roof down. And she actually felt respect for him. It didn't suit a Thakore to be calm all the time. Look at her son Gajendar. He was always cool. It wasn't a sign of a strong male personality, in the old matriarch's opinion. She was glad to know that Indrajeet was more like his grandfather, her husband, who was renowned for his black temper. She smiled despite the shouting she was receiving from the boy as she looked around at all the family members who were home. Meghnath stood on one side; his head hung in shame.

"Grandma, that child is barely two. Can you imagine the trauma she could have undergone if she had realised what was actually happening? It was lucky that the other lady was also there..."

"Who was this?" Grandma asked Meghnath, hoping to distract Indrajeet from a full-blown tirade.

"That was Sia Rathod, the salon manager at Maharaja International." Meghnath's reply was prompt.

There were matching scowls on Santhini Devi's and Dayanita's faces when they heard this. "What the hell was that woman doing in the car? How did she get in?" asked Grandma.

"Is that the point?" Indrajeet snarled; his eyes red with temper. "It was because Sia was there that Aarya wasn't upset..."

"Yes, that's true, Rajmata." Meghnath interjected.

Indrajeet continued, "Grandma, we spoke about this the day before yesterday. You promised me you wouldn't go ahead with this stupid idea of yours. I..."

Santhini Devi gave a nod of agreement. "I had decided not to go ahead with the idea, Indrajeet. I accepted your logic and even told you I would take up your offer. I promised you actually..."

"And who was going to inform Meghnath about it?" Indrajeet had grilled Meghnath on their way home. The other man had told him the whole story of how they had been planning this for over six months.

"Look Indrajeet. What has happened has happened. We can't do anything to undo it. I..."

"Pappa." Indrajeet cut his grandmother mid-sentence to turn and appeal to his father. "How unfair is this? It was lucky that Ritvik knew about the kidnap of his child almost immediately, as Sia informed him the moment Meghnath took the child in the car. We went into action promptly before the anxiety could actually build up. But just think how anxious a father would be if his little girl went missing. How could Grandma do this to the man? And he treats us all as his friends."

Gajendar nodded, in full agreement with his son. But what the hell could he do? His mother listened to no one and went about things exactly the way she wanted to, never bothering to consult with anyone in the family. This wasn't the first time she had brought shame to the family. He sighed. "I know exactly what you mean, Jeet. But how are you going to tackle your grandmother? She never listens..."

"How dare you both talk about me as if I am not around?" Santhini Devi jumped from her chair—it wasn't an easy feat considering her bulk—to shout at Gajendar and Indrajeet.

"Grandma, there was a time when you demanded respect. Now it's time you learn to command it, that is, if you want to be respected by any of us. This is the utmost limit. What if Ritvik goes to the police? He has a picture of the license plate of our car which has been registered in your name. He saw for himself that Meghnath kidnapped his daughter. A lot of people know that he's worked as your bodyguard. You could go to jail for this, you know?" Indrajeet didn't mince his words.

Santhini Devi paled as she plopped back into her sofa. "I..."

Dayanita went and sat next to her grandmother, her arm around the old woman's shoulders. "I think that's enough Jeet. Ritvik is too nice a man to..."

"Exactly my point. He's too nice a person. Why the hell would you both do this to him?" Indrajeet refused to calm down.

The threat of police had truly shaken Santhini Devi. She had always run wild, but had never got caught. Never thinking too much about the consequences, she had had her own way in everything. But it looked like she had crossed the limit this time round. "I will talk to Ritvik Bansal and maybe apologise to him..."

"He has threatened to hand you and Meghnath over to the police if either of you step into his territory." Indrajeet finally calmed down to give his grandmother a sly look. She was going to apologise to someone for probably the first time in her life.

Santhini Devi wanted to protest that Ritvik Bansal's territory used to belong to the Thakores until a few years ago. But she was smart enough to realise that her arguments would get her nowhere as the man had paid them way more than what the property had been worth in the market.

"Connect me to him on the phone, Indrajeet. I'll speak to him."

"Good girl!" Indrajeet grinned at the scandalised look on his grandmother's face.

S ia packed and left, after sending a letter of resignation to the HR department of Maharaja International. Since she was still under probation, she could get away with forfeiting a month's salary in lieu of notice. After thinking long into the night, she had arrived at the conclusion that it was best she went far away from the two people she loved the most. She could never face life if either Ritvik or Aarya felt ashamed of her. And that's what they would be if they ever got to know the truth about her past.

She called Kamini Sachdev to inform her that she was moving on without giving her a reason. "Where do you plan to go?" asked the concerned Kamini. The sensitive woman had sensed her agony from Sia's voice. How she wished the girl could find happiness! But it wasn't the right time yet, it seemed.

"I'm thinking of visiting my father and brother for a brief spell. They live in Dholpur. And after that," Sia shrugged, "I'll keep you informed, madam."

"You do that, Sia. But tell me something. Didn't you like the job at Maharaja International?"

"It wasn't bad, madam. But the pressure was more than I could take." Well, it wasn't exactly a lie, was it? She didn't need to confess to the other lady where the pressure came from.

"Oh, okay. Then it's a good thing for you to move on. I wish you all the best, Sia. I'm sure you will get another job soon. I will tell you if I get to know of any vacancy in your line. Do be in touch."

"Sure madam. Thank you. Bye."

Sia's eyes were dry when she caught the train to Dholpur, a single suitcase in her hand. There was no need to cry. She should actually feel happy, shouldn't she, for having met Ritvik and loved him; and Aarya, whom she had never dreamt of setting eyes on, ever again during this lifetime? Then why wouldn't her heart accept her logic? Sia stared at the countryside flying past the window, refusing to look into the hollowness of her future.

Eknath looked at the stylish stranger who walked into his home, unable to recognise the seventeen-year-old who had got married and left eight years ago. Yes, Sia had never been back to her parents' home, not even when her mother died. How could she have faced anyone from back home, with the kind of life she had been living during those days? "How are you, Pappa?"

"I am fine, Sia. How have you been?" He knew she wasn't with her husband any more, but had no idea about the reason for it. Sia had no plans to tell him either. They had drifted too far apart.

"I'm also fine Pappa. I hope you don't mind if I stay with you for a few days."

"What is this, Sia? Isn't this your house too?"

Sia gave him a small smile, keeping her suitcase in a corner. "Where's Shyam?"

"He has gone to college. He should be home in the evening. Wait, let me get some tea for both of us."

Sia looked at her father with wonder as he heated the tea he had already made, before pouring it into two small glasses. Handing her one, he sipped from his own. They chatted on and off, like lost relatives who were meeting after a long time, which was the truth in their case.

Sia refused to dwell on either her past or her future as she decided to spend time with her father and brother, giving them her complete attention.

Kamini Sachdev picked up her phone when it rang from a strange number approximately twenty-four hours after she had spoken to Sia.

"Hello, is it Mrs Kamini Sachdev? My name is Ritvik Bansal. Could you please spare me a few minutes, ma'am? I'd like to meet you as soon as possible."

Why was the name familiar? Kamini tried to recall, but couldn't. Curious, she agreed. "Can you come over today?" When the man agreed, she gave him her address. "I will expect you at seven in the evening."

"Sure, ma'am. I'll see you at seven."

The earlier day, Ritvik had contacted the private nursing home to find out details of Sia Rathod only to hit a road block. They had refused to share any details of the surrogate mother. "She has been sworn to secrecy, Mr Bansal, the same as you were. We can't divulge her details."

Ritvik left, wondering how he could go about it. He recalled that there was someone from a women's NGO who had been involved. If he went to ask the nursing home about it, they wouldn't tell him for sure. What to do now? Ritvik suddenly snapped his fingers. Santhini Devi wielded a lot of power even today. And the woman sure owed him one. He drove to the Thakores' home directly from the nursing home and walked through the open door.

"Hey man, welcome to our home." Rajvardhan greeted Ritvik with a handshake. "Have you come to kick my grandma's ass?" He enquired with a mischievous grin on his face.

Ritvik's laugh was strained. "Not really, though it's Santhini Devi I've come to meet."

"Come along." Rajvardhan guided Ritvik to the other end of the hall before turning left. "Grandma, see who has come to meet you." He so loved to drop a cat among the pigeons.

"Hello Mrs Thakore," Ritvik greeted her politely. She had truly surprised him by apologising profusely over the phone.

"Welcome, Ritvik. Sit down. Rajvardhan, ask Meghnath to serve us tea."

"Are you sure you aren't going to poison me, Mrs Thakore? Especially since you are asking Meghnath to serve us?" Ritvik couldn't help taking a dig at the old matriarch.

Rajvardhan stopped in his tracks as he doubled up with laughter while Santhini Devi had the grace to turn red in the face. "Of course not, Ritvik. Anyway, you don't have to take my word for it. The tea will be poured from the same pot. You can drink yours after I have tasted mine."

Ritvik tilted his head in agreement. "Actually, I need your help."

"Tell me, I owe you one."

"Exactly what I thought."

"Are you being cheeky with me, young man?"

Ritvik grinned. "I suppose."

"So, what do you want from me?" asked Santhini Devi who couldn't help being impressed by Ritvik's attitude.

"I need the name and phone number of..." He told her quickly what he required. "Do you think you will be able to get it for me?"

"There's no one in this city who will say no to me," said Santhini Devi, the touch of arrogance back in her voice. "You'll have the information within half an hour."

Santhini Devi looked at the hotelier as they sat there sipping tea and munching on homemade cookies. The nursing home was going to call her back in a short while. Taking a bold step, Santhini Devi asked Ritvik outright, "You know Dayanita, of course.

I am thinking you would make her a wonderful husband. What do you say?"

Ritvik bit his tongue as he was about to give the matriarch a rude response about what exactly he thought about her granddaughter. Changing his mind, he said mildly, "Thank you, Mrs Thakore. But I love someone else."

She eyed him curiously, accepting finally that Ritvik and Dayanita were not meant for each other. Why had he chosen to have a surrogate child if he loved someone? Strange man! Probably it was for the best that Dayanita wouldn't have to spend the rest of her life with him.

Ritvik had Kamini Sachdev's name and number when he left the Thakores' residence after twenty minutes.

Ritvik went by his private jet to Jhunjhunu, promising Aarya that he would be back the same night. He knocked on Kamini Sachdev's bungalow at exactly seven o' clock. A servant opened the door, inviting him to sit on the sofa in the living room.

Ritvik sat down only to get up immediately when he saw a lady walk down the staircase. "Hello ma'am, I'm Ritvik Bansal."

"Hello Mr Bansal. I am Kamini Sachdev. Before we begin, would you like to have something to drink? Maybe some juice?"

"That would be nice, Mrs Sachdev, thank you."

They settled down on adjacent sofas before Kamini said, "Tell me, how can I help you?"

"I came to talk to you about Sia Rathod. She..."

Kamini snapped her fingers as she recalled in what context she had heard Ritvik Bansal's name. He was the father of the surrogate baby which Sia had mothered. Why had he come to meet her? Without revealing her thoughts, she nodded. "Go on."

Curious about why the lady had snapped her fingers suddenly, Ritvik continued, "Sia Rathod is the surrogate mother of my daughter. I believe it was you who had suggested her as the candidate for the same."

"That's right. But how did you get to know her identity? She had been sworn to secrecy. And I can't believe that Sia would break a promise, ever."

Ritvik smiled when he heard the lady take Sia's side. He quickly explained the circumstances of how Sia had gone to work for him and later discovered that Aarya was his daughter.

"Oh, okay. You are the CEO of Maharaja International." It was a statement.

Surprised, Ritvik asked her straight out, "How did you know?"

Kamini looked at the man sitting in front of her. He was obviously a very big shot. Now why would he come to her for information about Sia unless he had a personal interest in the girl? "Before I tell you how I guessed it, you must tell me something, Mr Bansal. Why do you want to find Sia? Just now, I don't think she wants to be found."

Ritvik got up from the sofa with a jerk, shoving his hands into the pockets of his trousers. He took a few steps down the hallway before walking back towards

Kamini. "I've fallen in love with my child's mother and I want to marry her."

Kamini smiled, her eyes lighting up. "Did you tell Sia that?"

"More than once." Ritvik sighed deeply, his lips drooping.

"No wonder she ran away."

"What?!" Ritvik sat down with a thud on the sofa he had just vacated. "I don't think I understand."

"Ritvik," She paused, looking at her guest with a twinkle in her eyes, "I hope you don't mind my calling you by your first name. You don't know how glad I am that you have come to meet me today. Just tell me one more thing. How much do you know of Sia's past?"

Ritvik smiled first at Kamini's words before a look of enquiry came into his eyes. "I don't know much, to be truthful. I know she has finished school and is from Dholpur. I also know that she managed to do a beautician course in London. Oh, let me see." Light dawned in his eyes as he said, "She probably needed the money to do the course and that's why she had a surrogate child." He nodded to himself before continuing, "And well, Sia is my daughter's mother." He shrugged. "Does it really matter? I love the woman exactly as she is today."

"I am sure Sia fell in love with you too." Kamini's smile had widened into a happy grin. What a man!

"Obviously not enough to spend the rest of her life with me," Ritvik said bitterly.

"Don't lose heart, Ritvik. There's a reason why Sia behaved the way she did." Kamini understood now why Sia had quit her new job suddenly. "I think it's best if you stay for dinner as this is going to take some time." She called to a servant and instructed that the cook should make dinner for two. "My husband's not in town and it's just the two of us for dinner," she explained.

Ritvik waited silently, hoping she would give him Sia's contact address so he could be on his way.

Over the next couple of hours, Kamini told him Sia's story. She didn't leave anything out. If Ritvik planned to marry her, it was for the best that he knew the trauma Sia had undergone. If he didn't stop loving Sia after hearing all this—Kamini was sure he wouldn't—then her work was done. The very reason she had set up her NGO was to help the homeless and the downtrodden. If she had helped Sia climb out of the gutter, making sure she was completely healed, helped her set up a career and finally find love and happiness with a good, honest and decent man, then she would have achieved one hundred percent success.

Ritvik stopped eating his dinner midway when he heard how Sia had been molested by her own father-in-law. "Mrs Sachdev, please give me Sia's address. I need to see her urgently. Please." Ritvik, who had never had to plead for anything in his life, was ready to grovel at her feet by now.

"You might as well hear the rest of the story," insisted Kamini. Ritvik was in love with Sia today. What when they grew old? What if he got to know the rest of the story later? She wouldn't want him to stop loving Sia later on.

"Here you go." It was almost ten when she handed a sheet of paper with Sia's address on it. "How do you plan to get there?"

"I've got my private jet waiting at Jhunjhunu airport."

Kamini nodded. "The closest airport to Dholpur is Agra. You'll need to travel about a couple of hours by road before you reach her home. I would advise you to go tomorrow morning. People go to sleep early in small towns."

"Thank you so much, Mrs Sachdev. You have truly been a great help."

"As long as you don't forget to invite me to your wedding," said Kamini, a smile on her face.

Ritvik gave her his trademark grin which was free from tension for the first time since Sia had disappeared. "You bet." He gave Kamini a hug before leaving her house with a wave of his hand.

On the flight back to Udaipur, Ritvik couldn't stop thinking about Sia. What hell she had undergone at such a young age! And she believed that he wouldn't be able to accept her after hearing about her past. Ritvik swore to himself to convince her otherwise, even if it took the rest of their lives.

He couldn't wait for tomorrow to dawn. He told his pilot to keep the jet refuelled and ready to take off at 5.30 in the morning.

24

ia was bored and frustrated already on the second day at her father's home. It was obvious that both Eknath and Shyam had formed a routine which didn't include a third member. She felt like an extra thumb, totally useless.

She had never taken a break since her marriage and had been busy every day of her life. Sitting around, doing nothing was getting on her nerves, especially considering the mental state she was in. She missed Ritvik like one would miss a limb. And then there was Aarya. Though Sia had had very little chance to spend time with her daughter, it hadn't stopped her from getting attached to Aarya. Why was life so cruel? Hadn't she suffered enough before? Here she was, doing her best to make a success of her life, only to be thrown a googly once again.

Of all the salons in Udaipur, why did she have to go to work at Cleopatra's which belonged to her surrogate child's father? And why did she have to feel attracted to the man on first sight? Hadn't she had enough man trouble in her life? And over and above all that, Ritvik had to be the most adorable human being in the whole world, in Sia's perception.

Sia crossed her arms tightly around herself as she took the turn back home, returning from her morning walk. Yes, her father made tea for her in the mornings while her brother cooked breakfast. "It's alright Sia. You are on holiday. Let us continue to do the work around here." Eknath hadn't been very subtle with his remark, making Sia feel unwanted. She was seriously considering leaving the next day.

She pushed open the door which remained unlatched during the day and came to a sudden stop, her heart in her throat. She was surely hallucinating! Ritvik was sitting on a chair, holding a glass of tea in his hand.

"Good that you are back, Sia. Mr Bansal has been waiting for fifteen minutes," Eknath told his daughter.

Ritvik got to his feet, towering over Sia. "Do you wanna go for another walk with me?"

Giving a small nod, Sia turned and walked out of the door, totally aware of the man who followed close behind her.

They sat on a deserted park bench before Sia spoke in a rush. "I can't marry you, Ritvik."

"Why?" He traced a gentle forefinger down her silky cheek, stopping at the corner of her lips.

Sia turned her gaze, clouded with pain, to him. "Why won't you just accept what I'm saying? I can't marry you."

"I'll accept your decision if you insist that you *won't* marry me. Go on, say it!" Ritvik challenged.

Sia turned her face and buried it in his palm, her eyes tightly shut. Of course, she wanted to marry Ritvik. Of course, she wanted to live with him till the end of her life. Of course, she wanted to be Aarya's mother. Of course, she...

But when had her wants ever mattered to anyone?

Ritvik laughed softly, hugging her. "I did warn you there was no escaping me, didn't I?"

Sia moved away to look up at his handsome face with fire in her grey gaze. It looked like he wasn't going to accept her word for it. Maybe it was time for him to know the truth. And maybe he would leave her all alone after that. Only Sia didn't want to be left alone.

Ritvik decided to put Sia out of her misery. "I know all about your marriage to that bastard and the way his father treated you. I also know how Kamini Sachdev rescued you from the police and helped you get therapy. I know..."

Colour rushed into Sia's cheeks before draining away completely, leaving her pale, as expressions of horror and shame chased across her face. "How? How did you meet Kamini ma'am? I..."

"Sia, honey, listen. Does any of that matter? I know you had a bitter experience during your marriage. But I promise you that I'll always treat you with respect. I..."

Sia placed a hand over his mouth, stopping him mid-sentence. "That was never an issue. I know you'll never treat me badly. It's just that, Ritvik," her eyes pleaded with him to understand, "it's just that I am from the gutter. Let me be. I can't aspire to live the life of a queen. Once the fascination of a new relationship wears off, you won't fail to remember my roots. Believe me when I say you will hate me then." Sia turned her face away from him, not wanting him to see the tears shimmering in her eyes.

Ritvik rose up to stand tall in front of her. "How dare you?" His voice was a deep growl.

Sia looked up at him with a startled jerk. "What?" She didn't understand.

"How dare you think I have only a fascination for you? How dare you suggest it might wear off? I love you, Sia. I love the woman you are, the woman you have made yourself to be despite all the terrible experiences you underwent." He pulled her up into his arms, shaking her gently. "It wasn't your fault that those men behaved the way they did. It shows them in a bad light. How long do you plan to punish yourself? I want to cherish you, honey. I want to live a long and happy life with you. I want to have a couple of more kids with you, bring them up along with you this time round. I want you to be Aarya's mother, at least from now on. I want to belong to you. Will you make me yours?"

Was he for real?!

Tears ran down Sia's cheeks as she looked up at Ritvik's darling face, completely swayed by his passionate words. She laughed through her tears, pulling his head to press her forehead to his, whispering her answer, "Yes, please!"

The first thing that Ritvik did on returning to the hotel was to cancel Sia's resignation and reinstall her as the manager of Cleopatra's. They agreed that she would continue in the profession she had worked so hard at building.

And they had a grand wedding on the terrace of Maharaja International a month later, Ritvik pushing aside Sia's protests that it was her second time and, therefore, should be a quiet one. "What you call your first marriage is a farce, according to me. You were underage and hence it wasn't even fully legal. Just forget it. Our marriage is here, now. We are going to have the most fun." He had agreed to wait for a month only because he had been keen for Aarya and Sia to bond with each other during that time.

"But what would people think, say? We already have a two-year-old daughter." Sia looked at Ritvik with starry eyes. She was paying lip service only because she believed that someone had to tell him that. Nothing seemed to matter nowadays except his love for her which he showed her in many different ways.

"Who cares? Those who are our well-wishers will come to wish us anyway. The rest of the world doesn't matter, does it?"

Sia nodded, burying her face into her fiancé's neck.

And they all came: Ritvik's parents, his siblings, their partners, little Mehul, Meera Aunty, Sia's father and brother, Kamini Sachdev and her husband, the whole of the Thakore clan, every single employee of Maharaja International from the front office manager to the bell-hop and a horde of friends. Little Aarya was in her element, grinning from ear to ear, dressed in a stylish *gaghra choli* to attend her parents' wedding. There was *mehendi* and *sangeet* as well as the wedding. But during it all, Ritvik and Sia had eyes only for each other.

Sia was completely overwhelmed by the affection showered on her by her new family. It had been a tremendous relief to know that Ritvik had shared her background with them. It had made no difference to the way they treated her, unless she counted the admiration which they felt for her after knowing everything. She was glad that there was no need for her to feel ashamed of her past life. Ritvik had been right. Sia was convinced now that she was in no way responsible for the way Badal and his father had treated her.

Aarya didn't mind at all when her parents decided to go on a two-week honeymoon to the Maldives as she was going to be pampered by her grandparents who planned to stay back at the cottage which was fully renovated and was to be Ritvik and his family's home from now on. And then there were the kittens, not one or two but four of them, which Ritvik had gifted Aarya, who was excited beyond words. Ritvik had also insisted Meera Aunty stayed back with them, much to the woman's joy.

"So, Mrs Bansal, do you still want to escape from me?" Ritvik gave his wife an adoring look.

"Hmm... let me see." Sia looked at her husband, a mischievous look in her eyes as she ran her gaze over his handsome face. "Yeah, maybe when the sun starts rising from the west..."

Ritvik laughed, lifting Sia into his arms before he walked up the steps to get into the private jet which was taking them away to Maldives.

25

Sia didn't really know where the first ten days of their honeymoon had gone. They had lazed around on the private beach, soaking up the sun. Ritvik had taught her to swim. While she was still far away from being an expert, she could manage to survive if thrown into the water. She had been a tad hesitant when Ritvik made love to her on the beach in broad daylight the first time. "Ritvik, what if someone turns up?"

"What?" He grinned at her. "I'll cover you with my body so no one gets to see you naked." His black-as-sin eyes glinted mischievously as he kissed the pulse at her neck, a lazy hand sliding the strap of her bikini top.

Sia slammed a tight fist on his shoulder, pouting at him. "What if it's a woman and she sees you buck naked?"

Ritvik shrugged. "I don't mind." He burst out laughing when she pushed him down before sitting on his stomach, raining blows on his chest with both her fists now.

"But I do mind, okay?"

Ritvik removed the buckle that held her bikini top and flung it away, ogling at her breasts, before cupping them in his hands. "I want you."

Sia choked when she felt his thumbs stroke over the tips of her breasts rhythmically. Her eyes glazed over as she declared, "I want you too."

In the end, the owner of Maharaja International had his way with the queen of his heart with the sea, the sun and the sand bearing witness to their lovemaking.

THE END

BIBLIOGRAPHY

- *Organisational Behaviour in Hotels and Restaurants - An International Perspective* by Yvonne Guerrier.
- *Food and Beverage Service* - 5th edition by Dennis Lillicrap, John Cousins and Robert Smith.
- *The Catering Management HAND BOOK* (The Complete Guide to Hotel, Restaurant and outside catering) Edited by Judy Ridgway, Brian Ridgway
- *Effective Purchase Practices for Hotels and Restaurants in India* – F H & R A INDIA (November, 2003)
- *Guidelines and Incentives for Hotel Industry in India* – F H & R A INDIA (November, 2003)
- *Foods that Harm, Foods that Heal* – Published by Reader's Digest Association Limited

MORE BOOKS
BY
SUNDARI
VENKATRAMAN

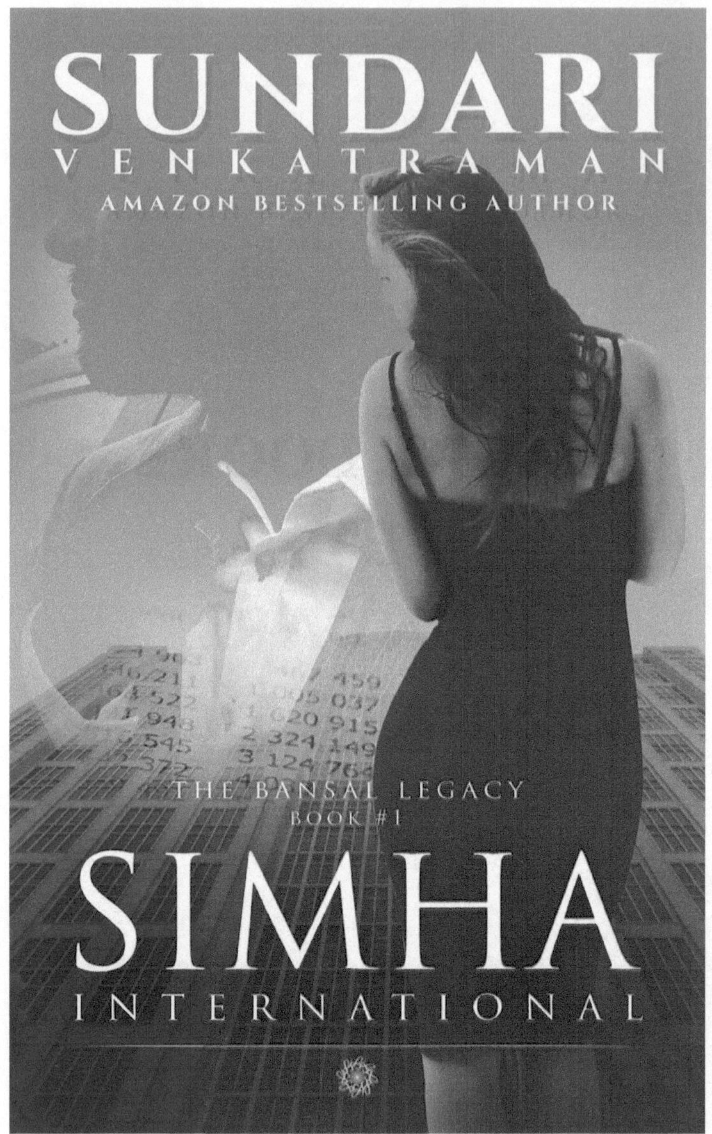

SUNDARI
VENKATRAMAN
AMAZON BESTSELLING AUTHOR
THE BANSAL LEGACY
BOOK #1
SIMHA
INTERNATIONAL

SIMHA INTERNATIONAL
(The Bansal Legacy #1)

Rohit Bansal, the handsome and suave managing director of Simha International, is the envy of many—from a director of the hotel to an employee.

A thief comes up with a simple modus operandi, believing that nobody's really going to find out anything about the thefts taking place. But when a guest brings it to his notice, Rohit is determined to save the reputation of Simha International and ropes in a top-notch detective. Will Rohit be able to find who the thief is before time runs out?

The lovely and intelligent Tasha Sawant goes to work at Simha International as the duty manager. Her experience in the hotel industry only adds to the hotel's excellent service.

Tasha is attracted to Rohit and it would seem that he reciprocates her feelings. Well, the lady isn't looking for a permanent relationship as it looks like she has already had an unpleasant experience. But then, what about the guy? Does Rohit want any kind of relationship with Tasha?

**Simha International* is the first book in The Bansal Legacy trilogy

SUNDARI
VENKATRAMAN
AMAZON BESTSELLING AUTHOR
THE BANSAL LEGACY
BOOK #2
ROSE GARDEN
INTERNATIONAL

ROSE GARDEN INTERNATIONAL
(The Bansal Legacy #2)

Interior Designer Jamie Scott from Australia feels a strange connection to Ooty, a hill station in South India—what one would say, 'a call of the soul'. Then there are those diaries that his grandmother had left behind. Jamie decides to go on a holiday to Ooty.

Rhea Bansal runs 5-star hotel Rose Garden International on oiled wheels, as its managing director. She finds herself at a loose end—as if there's no challenge left in her life.

And soon, the challenge walks into her life...

Will Rhea, with her broken relationships, be able to forge a new and lasting one, that too one that's interracial? Will she let anyone get close enough to reach her heart?

More complications set in though, in the form of a policeman and a politician.

Read the story to find out if the high-powered businesswoman from North India who has settled in the South and the laidback artist from Alice Springs in Australia can have a life together.

Rose Garden International is the second book in The Bansal Legacy trilogy

Mr. Perfect
SUNDARI VENKATRAMAN
Mr. Perfect
SUNDARI VENKATRAMAN

MR. PERFECT

Saloni Malhotra is miserable with her lonely and servile existence in Chicago, while her husband Dr. Manish Chawla is too selfish to be bothered about his wife's happiness. It's watching her sister's closeness to her new husband that actually opens Saloni's eyes to the lack in her life.

Aarav Chopra hasn't looked at another woman since he fell in love with the seventeen-year-old Saloni. The nine years in-between seem to disappear when he sets eyes on her again at her sister's wedding. But this time round, his love stretches to include her son too, as Mitesh holds not just Aarav's finger but also his heart in his little hand.

Things come to a head when she flees Chicago to return to Delhi along with her baby son Mitesh.

Life throws Saloni and Aarav together as she goes to work in his group of companies while awaiting her divorce. The attraction is as powerful as ever! But Saloni is absolutely clear that she wouldn't be tied to a man ever again.

Will Aarav be able to convince her otherwise?

Connect with Sundari Venkatraman here:

Sundari Venkatraman Books

Sundari Venkatraman Books

https://www.sundarivenkatraman.in

Author Sundari Venkatraman

@sundarivenkat

@sundarivenkatraman

sundarivenkat@gmail.com